P9-CQW-129

2 0 2 1 4 4 2 9 7

CHIDDIX JUNIOR HIGH SCHOOL

DATE DUE

DEC 07 2017			

Demco, Inc. 38-293

MY SEVENTH-GRADE LIFE IN TIGHTS

▲▲▲▲▲▲▲▲▲

MY SEVENTH-GRADE LIFE IN TIGHTS

BROOKS BENJAMIN

▲▲▲▲▲▲▲▲▲▲

Delacorte Press

Text copyright © 2016 by Charles Brooks Benjamin
Jacket art copyright © 2016 by The Little Friends of Printmaking

All rights reserved. Published in the United States by Delacorte Press, an imprint of Random House Children's Books, a division of Penguin Random House LLC, New York.

Delacorte Press is a registered trademark and the colophon is a trademark of Penguin Random House LLC.

randomhousekids.com

Educators and librarians, for a variety of teaching tools, visit us at RHTeachersLibrarians.com

Library of Congress Cataloging-in-Publication Data
Benjamin, Brooks.
My seventh-grade life in tights / Brooks Benjamin. — First edition.
p. cm.
Summary: "All Dillon wants is to be a real dancer. And if he wins a summer scholarship at Dance-Splosion, he's on his way. The problem? His dad wants him to play football. And Dillon's freestyle crew, the Dizzee Freekz, says that dance studios are for sell-outs" — Provided by publisher.
ISBN 978-0-553-51250-2 (hc) — ISBN 978-0-553-51251-9 (glb) — ISBN 978-0-553-51252-6 (ebook)
[1. Dance—Fiction. 2. Dance teams—Fiction. 3. Competition (Psychology)— Fiction. 4. Middle schools—Fiction. 5. Schools—Fiction.] I. Title.
PZ7.1.B4535My 2016
[Fic]—dc23
2014049045

The text of this book is set in 12-point Berling.
Jacket design by The Little Friends of Printmaking
Interior design by Trish Parcell

Printed in the United States of America
10 9 8 7 6 5 4 3 2 1
First Edition

For Jackie. For everything.

▲▲▲▲▲▲▲▲▲▲

I stared deep into the world of two-faced backstabbery. And it was all inside my phone.

I never would've found the website on my own, but I'd set a Google alert about a month earlier for *become a real dancer*. I'd also set up one for *ninja movie audition* and *free concert in Sunnydale*, but those never gave me anything useful.

This alert was different. I leaned against the bathroom sink and scrolled down the page. Dance-Splosion, the biggest dance studio in east Tennessee, was giving away a three-week summer scholarship in June to one lucky dancer. And this was the last week they were taking submissions.

At the bottom was a picture showing a wall of their

dancers, each one posing like the show had just ended and the crowd was cheering so hard the ceiling was about to cave in.

I imagined my name in a Broadway show program:

Introducing twelve-year-old Dillon Parker, dancing some awesome style and definitely not the lame ninja freestyle one he made up.

Below the picture was the Dance-Splosion slogan: *Where* real *dancers are made.*

Those five little words had me trapped in a bathroom with my crew waiting for me outside.

A *real* dancer.

Every time I thought about it, my stomach twisted into a knot. But there was no way I could go through with it. Not without hating myself afterward.

"Dillon, you almost finished?" Kassie's voice crept in through the door crack and yanked me back to earth.

I shoved the phone into my pocket. "Um, yeah. Just need to, um—flush." I pushed the lever on the toilet, ran the water for a minute, and opened the door into my den.

"Dude, we thought you fell in or something," Austin said, standing behind his camera, cleaning his glasses on his shirt. "Kassie was about to send Carson in to pull you out of the plumbing."

Kassie laughed. "Okay, we've got time for one more run-through." Her eyes landed on me. "You up for it?"

"Yeah. Definitely."

She pulled her jet-black hair into a ponytail. One curl fell down over her forehead. It always did that. Like that one bit of hair refused to go along with the rest. That was totally Kassie. A rebel. Some of the kids had teased her when she first moved here from Haiti. But she'd never let them bother her.

"All right, we're rolling," Austin said, then glanced at the lights flickering above us. "Hold on."

Carson let out a loud groan. "Perfect. Last practice before school starts and we're going to look like we're dancing in a lightning storm." His entire body perked up. "Ooh, that might actually be cool. Let's start before it turns normal again."

"Trust me, it looks terrible," Austin said. "We need to invest in some lights. This place is a cave. And don't get me started on the smell. It's like someone farted in an old shoe."

"The lighting's fine," Kassie said.

Austin poked his head out from behind his camera. "Oh, sorry. I thought *I* was the director." Carson opened his mouth, but Austin cut him off before he could speak. "Come on, guys. I already feel stupid recording these. It's not like y'all can't just do it yourselves. Let me at least make it look good."

Austin was right. He recorded all of our routines even though we really didn't need him to. But he said he'd let us all be zombies in a short film he was making next summer. That was enough to convince us he should help out.

"How long will it take before the light stops?" Kassie asked.

Austin grabbed a pillow and tossed it at the ceiling. It smacked against the clear plastic cover and the light instantly stopped flashing. Austin let out a quick laugh like he was surprised it had worked.

We got into our first position, squished together closer than we should've been. My den was pretty small, even with the furniture pushed out of the way. Austin hit play on Kassie's phone and the room filled with a low, electronic bass groove.

Kassie moved first, flying into a perfect triple spin. She was a blur, twirling at sonic speed.

Next up was Carson. He jumped, his long, skinny legs stretched out into a perfect split. I couldn't have drawn straighter lines with a ruler.

I was next.

I closed my eyes and let the song pour into my muscles. Just like Kassie had taught me. I pretended the top of my head opened up on a hinge and the music filled every empty space inside me. And then . . .

A deep breath.

Feel the music.

Become the music.

Let the lid snap shut.

And take off.

I did a spin-drop, landing on my knees and windmill-ing my arms. I used the momentum to pop right back up and unleash a set of moves I had pieced together from some of my favorite dance movies and kung fu flicks. Jumps, kicks, twists, punches, a little pop and lock—I tried it all. My dad always says it looks like I'm having a seizure when I dance, but what does he know? The most dancing I'd ever seen him do was when he dropped a paint can on his toe last year.

My karate action didn't really seem out of place most of the time. They were the only moves I was good at, so Kassie always made sure our routines had some sort of fighting part to them. They had to, or I wouldn't have had anything to do. I'd just have been a statue in the background while the other dancers did all the cool moves.

My first few punches and kicks felt great.

But that's where the *epic* ended and the *epic fail* began.

The more I saw Kassie and Carson flow across the floor like a pair of dance swans, the more I felt like I was just flailing around, trying to keep up. So I threw my weight to the side, planting one hand on the floor for a one-handed cartwheel. I'd seen Kassie and Carson do it a million times. It couldn't be that hard.

But my elbow buckled and I crashed to the floor, smacking Kassie's shoulder with my foot.

"Ow!" Kassie's hand flew to her arm.

"Cut!" Austin yelled, stopping the music. "Dude, what're you doing?"

I scrambled to my feet. "I'm so sorry! Kass, are you okay?" Great. I finally muster up the courage to try an actual dance move and I end up breaking our best dancer.

"Everyone all right?" my mom called downstairs. "I heard a scream."

"We're fine, Mrs. Parker. Thanks," Kassie yelled. She worked her shoulder around, then asked me, "What happened? Did you trip or something?"

"I think he was going for a roundoff." Carson dragged his hand through his blond hair. He turned to Austin. "Or did he just fall again?"

Austin shrugged. "All I saw was a foot flying through the air. And not in a cool way."

I sat on the back of the couch. "I'm sorry. I just wanted to do something besides punch and kick all over the place."

"Why?" Kassie asked. "You're awesome at punching and kicking."

"Yeah, only because I don't know how to do anything else."

Carson took a drink from his water bottle. "But that's sort of your thing."

"I don't want my thing to *just* be punches and kicks, though. I wanna be able to do moves like you two, but you won't teach me."

"Not again," Austin mumbled, slapping the screen closed on his camera.

Kassie hopped up beside me. "I asked you to join us because you were doing all those karate moves, remember?"

I did. It was the first week of sixth grade. She'd found me after school practicing the kata I had to remember for my green belt. I'd told her I wasn't dancing.

She'd told me I really was.

"The whole reason I started this crew was to make a statement," she said now. "That dance isn't about rules and technique. It's about expression."

"But I've gotta start learning some real moves eventually." I looked up at Carson. "You're not the only one who wants to go pro one day, you know."

His eyes dropped. I hoped it was because he felt sort of bad for not helping me more and not because he knew no choreographer would hire someone with a fake dance style.

"I don't even wear real dance clothes. I mean, why am I the one who has to dance in jeans? Can I at least wear my football pants or something?"

"Yeah, let him wear those," Austin said. "It's about time they saw some action."

"You're funny, Austin," I replied. But he was right. The only action my football pants ever saw was when I got a splinter in my butt last year after I sat down on the bench. I wasn't even sure why I stayed on the team.

"Our clothes are our uniform. It's another way we express ourselves," Kassie said. "Three different dance styles, three different uniforms. I already told you to buy some baggier jeans."

"Yeah, my dad said I didn't need another pair." I fell back onto the couch cushions, staring up at the light that had started flickering again. "Guess I'm stuck being the fake dancer with the wedgies."

Kassie slid down beside me. "Look, the fact that you don't have all that technique is *why* we love your dancing. Me and Carson went through the brainwashing at our studios. Which is why I only have one rule: studios are for sellouts. They're all business, and dancing's all art."

Carson leaned over, staring down at me. "In a way, you're lucky. When you dance, you don't have to worry about lines and feet and hands. You just get out there and move."

"Exactly!" Kassie said. "You just need to keep doing the moves that feel right. The moves that fit. Your dancing is pure. Which makes it awesome."

It felt great to hear her say that. But I was tired of *pure*. *Pure* was just another way to say *You have no idea what you're doing, but thanks for making us look good.*

Austin held his phone out over my head. "Hate to break up the group hug, guys, but my mom's here."

Kassie's shoulders dropped. "All right. We'll pick back

up on Saturday. Before we go"—she sat up on her knees and put her hand out, palm down—"let's make our promise."

Carson put his hand in. Austin was next. I peeled myself off the couch seat and lifted my hand, letting it hover over everyone else's.

"The crew comes first."

That was the oath. The promise we made every practice.

I could practically hear the dancers on the Dance-Splosion website whispering inside my pocket. Wondering what I was going to do. Betting on whether I was going to end my summer with a big, fat lie.

Kassie's eyes narrowed. "Everything okay?"

"Uh, yeah." My hand fell on the pile. "Everything's good."

Kassie was the last one to leave. She took a few steps up the stairs and stopped.

"I just—I hope you know I really do love your dancing. Like, a lot."

"Thanks, Kass. I love yours, too. A lot."

I pretended to smooth down my hair, hoping my hand would hide the ball of pink my face was turning into.

"Cool. You need help with the couch?"

"Um, no. I'll get it. Thanks."

She waved and left.

My crew was my family. But they didn't understand

what it was like for me. The more we danced together, the more I felt like I didn't belong. Kassie and Carson had chosen to leave their studios. I'd never even set foot in one.

I was the outsider in a group of outsiders.

My chest ached at the thought of what I was considering. As soon as the door upstairs closed, I pulled the website up on my phone.

Dance-Splosion. Where *real* dancers were made.

Don't do it, my brain screamed. *Studios are evil, and you're evil for just thinking about doing this!*

My eyes stayed glued to the screen. Before I knew it, I was selecting a song from my playlist: "We Will Rock You" by Queen.

I pushed play and switched to video mode. I sat my phone on the coffee table and hit record.

"Hi, my name's Dillon Parker. I'm twelve years old and I go to Sunnydale Middle. I hope you like my dance."

▲▲▲▲▲▲▲▲▲

Every step I took down the hallway sent me deeper into a gigantic pit of regret.

I hadn't actually sent the YouTube link to Dance-Splosion. But the fact that I'd even thought about it made me feel like a traitor.

Everyone was heading toward the gym for our first-day celebration assembly. Calling the first day of school a celebration was like calling a trip to the dentist a vacation. The only good thing about the first day back was that it was already Thursday.

Austin caught up with me on my way. "Hey, Dill," he said, taking a bite of a chicken biscuit. "You heading to— What's wrong?"

"Just wishing I didn't have to be here."

"I know what you mean. Some eighth grader corn-dogged me on my way to breakfast. I'm gonna have a butt bruise for a month."

"It's not that. It's . . . something else."

"What's up?"

I stopped at a bank of lockers, letting my head fall against the wall. I winced as the back of my skull clipped a padlock. For a second I thought about doing myself a favor and just knocking myself out.

Austin brushed a field of crumbs off his shirt. "If it's about your schedule, I feel you. I got Mrs. Kellerman for history." He put his hand to his neck, pretending to choke.

I closed my eyes. A million different answers scrambled through my brain, each one sounding worse than the one before it. I wanted to tell someone. I'd bottled up my secret for less than a day and it already wanted to escape. Austin was my best friend. If anyone would understand, he would.

"I messed up. Like, for real," I said.

Austin slid his finger under his glasses to scratch his eyelid. "Okay. What'd you do this time?"

I took a deep breath and sighed. "I recorded an audition video to a contest Dance-Splosion is having."

"Dance-Splosion? As in Kassie's old dance studio? Why would you do that?"

"I have no idea. I think I was sick of not getting help. It just all happened really fast."

"Dude, Kassie's gonna go ballistic when she finds out."

"That's the thing. I never sent the link to them."

"Oh. Then why are you worried?"

"Because I *thought* about sending it in! What does that mean?"

He put a hand on my shoulder. "It means you didn't send it in. And she won't find out. So stop worrying about it."

Maybe he was right. Maybe I didn't have anything to worry about. But then why did I still feel so bad? "No. I have to tell her. I'll do it fast. Like tearing off a Band-Aid. I owe her that at least." I pushed myself off the lockers, back into the hallway traffic.

"Do that, then. Hey, why didn't you get me to record it for you?"

"Well, I—because you already left. I should have, though. You would've talked me out of it."

"Nah, I'm just the director. I only tell you things like stop judo-kicking yourself out of the frame." Austin took another bite, dropping a chunk of biscuit on the floor. "So what's up? I thought you loved dancing with them."

"I do, Austin. It's just . . . I don't know." I shook my head. "When Kassie showed us the new choreography, I thought I was gonna learn all these new moves. But all she wanted me to do was the same old stuff. Then Carson started talking about entering us in a dance competition."

"Dude, you were the one who got all excited about competing."

"I know. But that was before I realized I was the only one not getting any better. And don't act like you haven't noticed."

Austin shot me a *What did I do?* look. "So? You heard Kassie. All she cares about is that you're expressing yourself. Even if you did almost kick her arm off."

"Shut up, Austin. Besides, that's easy for her to say. She already dances like an angel."

Austin laughed, spraying a mist of chicken everywhere. "Aww, you're so romantic."

We walked into the gym. Most of the football players usually sat together during assemblies. But I never did, since I was on the blue team. Which was the group right below second string. We were basically glorified tackling dummies.

I stopped at the edge of the bleachers and spotted Kassie standing about halfway up, waving her arms at us. I followed Austin up the steps. Kassie scooted over to give me a spot to sit. Before my butt even hit the bleacher seat—

"Hi, my name's Dillon Parker. I'm twelve years old and I go to Sunnydale Middle. I hope you like my dance." She was watching my audition video on her phone.

I grabbed the edge of the bleachers so hard my knuckles popped. I tried to speak, but I was too busy almost-hyperventilating. I must have forgotten to make the video private. And now the entire world could see it. Even worse—Kassie!

My chest tightened. This couldn't be happening. I thought about throwing myself down the bleacher steps and playing the pity card. But I was frozen, watching my routine and wondering how bad Kassie was going to hate me for it.

The video played through to my last move—a double twist with a roundhouse kick. I'd caught so much air I thought I was gonna ram my head through the ceiling. I'd gotten in an extra half spin. As the song hit its final big note, I landed with my fist way over my head.

With the backside of my jeans ripped.

And staring right back at me and the other 1,594 people who had watched the video was the slightly sweaty pair of bright white underwear I'd been wearing.

The blood drained from my head and the entire gym started to spin. I retraced my steps, trying to figure out how I didn't notice my butt was practically hanging out during my dance.

1. Everyone left and I recorded my video.
2. My mom yelled at me to come upstairs for dinner.
3. I jumped in the shower while it uploaded.
4. I deleted the evidence from my phone.

I buried my face in my hands. I'd never even watched the routine.

Austin barked out a loud laugh. "Dude, you still wear briefs!"

There wasn't time for me to give him a dirty look. I was already halfway to a faint.

"Stop it, Austin. This is serious." Kassie turned, staring at me. "What's this for, Dillon?"

Lie. Lie to her and just say it was for fun and it was nothing and she should just forget about the whole thing forever. That was all I had to say. And she'd probably believe me. She'd probably even laugh and say it was a cool idea that I "put myself out there."

So what did I do?

I confessed.

"Dance-Splosion is having a contest for a scholarship and I recorded an audition, but I never sent them the link, I swear! I don't know what I was gonna do with it." I probably broke the speed record for spilling my guts, but at least it was out there. Fast like a Band-Aid. Still hurt, though.

Kassie didn't say a word. She just looked at me, her eyes wide. I couldn't stand it. I shoved my face against my palms and prayed she wouldn't hate me for the rest of my life.

When she finally did say something, it wasn't what I was expecting.

"Oh my gosh, I just had the best idea ever."

My head popped back up. Kassie was staring at the screen with this open-mouth grin on her face. Me and Carson shared a quick look, probably wondering why our crew leader wasn't tearing me a new one.

"I'm serious, guys, this is so good."

Carson waved his hand in front of her face. "Earth to Kassie. We can't read your mind, sweetie."

"Oh. Yeah, sorry." She took a deep breath and re-played the video. "Okay, so think about this. What if Dillon *did* send in the video—" Her hand shot up to cut me off. "And if he gets picked, he'll have to accept the award or dance onstage or whatever the winner does, right? So if that happens, right when he's got everyone's attention, he lets them have it."

"Lets them have it?" Carson asked.

"Yeah! He can be all like, *You can keep your lousy dance rules and your lousy dance studio!*" She dropped an in-visible mike and looked at me. "What do you think?"

"Hold up, you mean you're not ticked off at him?" Austin asked.

I shot Austin a *Would you please shut up before you actually do make her mad?* glare. "I was never gonna send them the link, Austin." I turned to Kassie. She had one eyebrow cocked like she only halfway believed me. "Please believe me. Studios are for sellouts. That's the rule."

Austin's eyes grew huge behind his massive lenses. "Hold up, Kassie—you're not being serious, are you?"

"I am. I think it's time we send the studios a message." Her eyes fell on someone sitting in the bottom row. I knew who she was looking at the second she did it.

Sarah Middleton.

The eighth-grade photography club president and Dance-Splosion's best dancer. Kassie never talked about why she'd dropped out, but I had a pretty good feeling it had something to do with Sarah.

"Okay, I am *so* voting we do this," Carson said. "Remember last year when I went through my photographer phase? I took all these awesome pictures of the football team. There was one of DeMarcus that could've been an ad for Gatorade. It was that good. I emailed it to Sarah's club and she replied that it was inappropriate for me to be taking pictures of her boyfriend. She told everyone I was making DeMarcus uncomfortable."

"Well, you were obsessed with the guy," Austin said.

"What do you mean *were?*" Kassie added, winking at Carson.

He shook his head. "I'm being serious. You don't know how humiliating it is to have to hear the principal talk to your parents about harassment." Carson stared down at his hands for a second, then sucked in a quick gasp of air. "Oh my gosh. Okay, my turn to be a genius. You know what else he should do?"

I shook my head. Partly to say *No, I don't* and partly

to say *No, please don't make me, because I'm sure I don't want to hear it, judging by the crazy look in your eyes.*

"You should totally get Sarah to help you."

My jaw unhinged and dropped to my feet. Austin slammed his hand against his chest, coughing. A shower of biscuit crumbs landed on a guy sitting two rows down. "You want Dillon to ask *her* for help?"

"Yes! Think about it," Carson said. "She probably knows all the judges. If she's helping him, then she'll do whatever she can to make sure he wins. You know how she is. All she cares about is winning."

Kassie drummed her feet on the bleacher in front of her. "This is so exciting!" She bumped her shoulder against mine. "I bet you didn't think this was going to happen, huh?"

"Yeah. Especially the part where I mooned the entire world. I told you jeans were a bad idea."

"Hey, don't worry about that." Kassie grabbed my hand. "Your dance was amazing. Don't listen to what everyone else is saying. We're all freaks here. And freaks have to stick together."

"Can I get an 'Amen'?" Carson said with his hands in the air. He waved off a few of the weird looks from the students around us. "Plus you should be proud. You've got a seriously cute butt."

"Ooh, he does, doesn't he?" Kassie added with a quick eyebrow waggle, which would normally make my arms go all goose-bumpy.

"Wha abow me?" Austin asked through a mouthful of biscuit. "I goh a cyoo buh?"

"What butt?" Kassie and Carson said at the same time, and burst into laughter. Austin rolled his eyes and shoved the last bite of food into his mouth.

"So what do you think? About the contest, I mean," Kassie asked softly. Just to me. Like she was giving me a chance to back out without anyone hearing.

My ears filled with the thudding of my heartbeat. Partly from having my face so close to hers. But partly because I had no idea what I was supposed to say. So I decided on "I'll, um—I'll think about it."

Finally, the sounds of middle school life slowly crept back into my head—including an explosion of giggles erupting from the row behind us. I looked back at everyone huddled around an iPad, glancing back and forth from the screen to me.

"Real mature, guys," Carson yelled.

"You gotta be kidding me," I groaned. One kid held up the iPad, the YouTube video zoomed in and paused at the spot where I underwear-mooned the entire world.

Kassie shot them a nasty scowl.

It took me a second, but I finally figured out what they were whispering.

My new nickname.

Tighty Whitey.

▲▲▲▲▲▲▲▲▲

Sometimes I hated the fact that my parents worked from home.

I never got to come back from school to an empty house like most kids with parents who had normal jobs. On most days, I walked in on some discussion about taxes or clients or whether or not there was enough money to cover some bill.

And there's nothing more awkward than watching your parents try to pretend nothing's wrong.

I grabbed the knob, listening through the door for a break in the conversation.

"I don't care how long you've known him, Chuck, you can't make a decision like that without me knowing!"

"I made it because his business idea was worth investing in. How long I've known Alan wasn't a factor."

"Why do I have a hard time believing that? You do realize three out of our last six investments were with your old college buddies, right?"

There was a pause. The eye of the parental storm. And my cue to come in.

I opened the door and kicked off my shoes. Mom and Dad instantly went rigid, putting on their best fake smiles. Mom was standing at the counter, pulling the stringy parts of the beans off, and Dad was sitting at the table, glancing back and forth from his phone to a stack of papers.

"Hey, sweetie. How was your first day?" Mom asked.

I wanted to say my day had been a gigantic wad of cruddiness. But I just grunted instead, hoping my parents would take the hint and let me crawl back to my room and smother myself with a pillow before dinner.

Dad got up and set his phone on the counter. "If you don't have much homework, I was thinking we could get you some new cleats. Your old ones are probably too small."

"I dunno," I said. "But I could use some baggy jeans."

Dad sighed. "I already told you, I'm not buying you baggy jeans so you can let your underwear hang out all day."

"And like I told you back, they're for dance. And trust me, I need them." I considered showing him my video. But then he'd probably just laugh and tell me that's why

I shouldn't dance. "Besides, I've been thinking about asking the coach if I could drop out of football this year."

Dad's head snapped up. "What? Why? You love football."

"Um, I sit on the bench every game."

Mom slid a pan out of the oven and shut the door. I got a whiff of the double-baked mac and cheese. Maybe I did have something to live for. "Well," she said, "I'm fine with you quitting."

"He's not quitting," Dad said.

"If he wants to, then why not? He needs to focus more on his schoolwork anyway."

"Carol, his grades are fine. Being on a team builds character."

"Like a dance team?" I said, totally getting ignored. Big surprise.

"Besides, I don't want him going through life thinking the way to solve problems is to quit."

"Unless it's dance," I added. No response.

"Chuck, you do realize football's just a sport, right?" Mom said. "Not a religious experience?"

"Obviously you've never seen the Titans play," he said, going back to his stack of papers.

As soon as I reached the stairs, they started right back up. Football. Taxes. Alan Scapelli. Luckily, my bedroom door muffled out most of the arguing.

I tossed my backpack on the bed and slumped down

into my desk chair, scanning my bookmarks tab still up on the screen. There were tons of free teach-yourself-to-dance tutorials I'd found on YouTube. I clicked on the last one I'd found—a video on different ways to do a hip-hop slide step.

Then I glanced at the search bar at the top.

"Don't do it," I mumbled. "It'll just make things worse."

My fingers slid onto the keyboard. I knew I shouldn't. But somewhere deep down I felt like I didn't have a choice. I had to face my technique-less demons. I swallowed what little pride I had left and pulled up YouTube. I typed *Dillon Parker dance* into the search bar.

There it was.

My heart stuttered. Three thousand views? How was that even possible? There weren't even three thousand people in Sunnydale. I let my head fall on my keyboard. No way people were going to forget about this. Getting flushed down the toilet would have been better than what I was going through. At least then I could've disappeared into the sewer and lived the rest of my life as some weird underground dancing hermit.

I pulled my head up. My nose must've clicked something and landed me on a different site. Good. The fewer views the video got, the better. It took me a second to notice I was looking at the Dance-Splosion photo archive.

Shots of dancers perched on one foot. Arms floating in graceful curves. Toes pointed like the tips of ninja swords. And right there in the middle of them all was a snapshot of Sarah Middleton, poised in mid-leap, defying gravity.

The double knots in my stomach slowly unraveled. Sure, the entire school was probably at home sharing the video of my underwear, putting it to different music tracks, adding in a whole library of gross sound effects for the big reveal at the end.

But they were watching the old Dillon Parker.

The one who was dancing without any hope of ever getting better.

I was the new and improved Dillon Parker.

The one who had just gotten permission to get some actual help from a destined-to-be-professional dancer.

My entire body tingled at the thought. Even though I'd recorded the video, the last thing I actually wanted was to become a studio sellout snob. But doing what Kassie had asked me to do wouldn't turn me into one. All I had to do was walk up to Sarah and ask. She wouldn't have any reason to help me. Eighth-grade club presidents don't associate with moppy-haired seventh graders with pimples on their chin. But I could probably find a way to convince her.

I scooted up in my seat, staring at her picture.

The chance of me actually getting good enough to

make it into a top-three spot was practically zero per-cent. Maybe even less. And even if I did win somehow, there was no way I'd choose a studio over my crew.

But I could walk away from this whole thing with an entire arsenal of new moves. Improved techniques. Maybe even an actual dance style. My moment of last-day-of-summer treachery had just unlocked a door for me. One that might be able to slingshot me to the top of any choreographer's list.

There was too much excitement pulsing through my veins for me to sit down. I hopped up out of my chair, pacing back and forth. My eyes were locked on Sarah.

Come to me, Tighty Whitey, she was saying. *Let me help you become a real dancer.*

Yep. That door was unlocking.

And I was about to ninja-kick the thing down.

4

▲▲▲▲▲▲▲▲▲

I dumped a mound of chicken pot pie onto my lunch tray, stepping back to avoid the splatter of brain-colored goo.

"I can't believe you're going through with it." Austin took the spoon from me and dug out his own mountain of slop. "And you're even gonna talk to Sarah? You really think she'll help you?"

"Not really," I said, wiping off the dots of chicken decorating my shirt. "I'm doing it for Kassie. I already texted her that I've made up my mind."

"Oh yeah, I'm sure this is all just for Kassie."

"Okay, fine. It's mostly for her."

We waited to punch in our lunch numbers at the register. Austin dabbed a wad of gravy around the mouth of a smiling plastic apple sitting beside the stacks of napkins. "This whole plan's a terrible idea. Like, an I-can-feel-it-in-my-guts sort of thing, dude." He tipped the apple over, adding in a sploochy sound effect.

"Austin, you heard Kassie. She *wants* me to go for that scholarship. This is sort of a win-win thing for me. I go along with Kassie and get some help from Sarah. When I don't make it in, I'm right back where I was. But with better lines."

"And if you actually *do* win? Something tells me you're gonna have a hard time just throwing away a dance scholarship."

"I'd do it for the crew. And you, since we're supposed to make your movie next summer."

"Whatever, dude," Austin said. "All you think about is dance. You even take notes when you watch *Dance Moms.*"

"There you go." I gave him a hard pat on the shoulder. "When it comes to dance, I'm more focused than anyone. Which is why this is gonna work."

We headed over to our table, where Kassie and Carson were already sitting. I could hear Austin mumbling behind me the whole way.

As soon as I sat down, Carson held a banana beside his face like it was a gun. "His name's Pahker. Dillon Pahker."

"Oh my gosh, your British accent is awful," Kassie said, laughing.

"Shut up, it was amazing and you know it." Carson peeled the little sticker off and stuck it on her forehead. "So, you ready to infiltrate the enemy lair, Dillon?"

As soon as he said it, a nervous pinch worked its way through my insides. "I guess." Austin let out a long sigh, mumbling something. I tilted my head toward him. "He's not exactly convinced this is a good idea, though," I added.

"Dude . . ." Austin shot me a look like I'd just told everyone he still has to have a night-light on when he sleeps.

"It's okay, Austin," Kassie said. "You can say what you're thinking."

Austin's eyes fell to his mashed potatoes. He took a deep breath. "It's just—Sarah's never really bothered us. It seems sort of mean."

"But we're not doing this to *her*. We're doing this to her *studio*." I looked at Kassie, half shrugging. "Right?"

"We're doing this to *both* of them," Carson said.

Kassie shook her head. "No, Dillon's right. We're sending a message to Dance-Splosion. Not to Sarah."

Austin stabbed his pot pie with his fork. "Whatever. You hate Sarah as much as Carson does."

"I don't hate Sarah. I hate Dance-Splosion."

"Fine. Then prove it. Tell us what they did that was so evil," Austin said. I shot him a quick glare, but he just glared right back and said, "I'm serious. If she wants you to go through with this, then you deserve to know why, right?"

I forced my eyebrows together a little harder, trying to look angrier. But I was starting to think Austin was right. I kind of wanted to know, too.

Kassie shrank back. I knew she was just going to shake her head and tell us to not worry about it. But then she spoke. "Okay, fine. A month before nationals, our teacher said she was only going to enter one solo for our age group. She picked Sarah just like she always did. But Sarah didn't want it. The teacher tried to talk her into it, but Sarah wouldn't budge. So it went to me. The teacher wasn't happy, but I was so excited. My first solo. I couldn't believe it." Kassie was smiling. Like she was feeling the excitement all over again. But then it faded and she slid her hands into the pocket of her hoodie. "The week before we left, our teacher pulled me from the competition. She said she'd decided to give the solo to Sarah."

Carson's mouth fell open. "And you *don't* hate her for that?" he asked. "She went behind your back and stole your chance at a national title."

"Sarah—" Kassie's mouth stayed open, but nothing more came out. Like the words were just stuck in her throat. "It's the studio's fault. They're the ones who let it happen."

Carson stole a baby carrot from Austin's tray. "Keep

telling yourself that if you want to. But I know better. That girl is made of evil."

Kassie bit her lip like she wanted to say something. But then she pushed a stray curl behind her ear and looked at Austin. "Satisfied?"

Austin's lips were pinched together and he was taking loud breaths through his nose. "Would it matter if I wasn't? It's not like I'm a part of the crew, anyway."

"Austin, yes, you are," Kassie said.

But Austin just shrugged and went back to mutilating his food.

"So what's the plan?" Carson asked. "And don't tell me you don't have one."

A tiny smile finally turned up the corners of Kassie's mouth. "Of course I have a plan." She slid a sheet of paper out into the middle of the table. It showed the same competition rules from the Dance-Splosion website that I didn't read the first time I saw them. "It says once you make it to the top three, you'll have to go to the studio and perform a solo for the teachers. They'll announce the scholarship winner at the Heartland Dance Challenge on November ninth."

"Oh, I danced there once!" Carson blurted out. "It's a really nice competition. Small, but everyone there was so sweet."

"Carson. Focus." Kassie pointed down the page a little. "Anyway, it says that at the Heartland contest, the finalists will perform one last solo for the audience. And since this is one of the last competitions of the season, tons of studios will be there."

"So what do I do?" I asked.

"I thought about writing you a speech."

"Yes! I want to help," Carson said. "We'll make it legendary."

"Well, don't get your hopes up," I said. "I probably won't make it that far."

One of Kassie's eyebrows popped up. "Why wouldn't you? You're an amazing dancer. Those judges would be stupid not to pick you."

I turned the paper over, expecting more to be on the back. And there was. But not a speech. "'Boogie Banditz. Rhythm Force. Dizzee Freekz.' What are these?"

"Oh yeah!" Kassie grabbed the paper out of my hands. "I came up with these last night. Crew names. If we're going to find a competition to dance in, we should have one. Carson and I already voted. I want you to pick which one you like."

She scooted the paper between me and Austin. He glanced at it and went right back to staring at his tray. "Why not just call yourselves the Anti-Sarah League?"

Carson laughed. "I kinda like that, actually."

I swatted Austin's arm, making sure he saw the unamused look on my face. I reread the names a few times and made my choice.

"Dizzee Freekz."

Kassie snatched the paper away, smiling. "That's what we chose, too!"

"Tell them how you came up with it," Carson said.

"Oh yeah! Okay, so you know my dad's Haitian and he speaks a ton of French. My mom's family is all from Greece. Well, *French* plus *Greek* equals *Freek*! Then I thought of the Dizzy Feet Foundation that Nigel's always talking about on *So You Think You Can Dance* and I got *Dizzee Freekz*! It's perfect!"

It *was* perfect.

And just like that we officially had our name: the Dizzee Freekz.

On my way to Mrs. Kellerman's history class, Sarah Middleton popped out of the bathroom with her two cheerleader besties, Red-Haired Barbie and Black-Haired Barbie. All three of them had their hair pulled back into ponytails, stretching their faces into tight half-surprised, half-irritated looks.

I stopped in the middle of the hallway. Students brushed by me on either side, tossing out my new nickname like it was a toll they had to pay just to walk by.

As soon as I took a step forward, a sharp pinch of pain zipped up my backside.

"'Sup, Tighty Whitey!"

I didn't have to turn around. The stench that crawled over my head told me who had a death grip on my underwear. Troy Pemberton, the Sunnydale Sharks' starting center. "Show me some of them moves, Parker!"

He wrenched my briefs up in his hand like he was wringing out a beach towel and then let go. The waistband snapped back into place and I stumbled forward, falling headfirst right into Sarah Middleton's chest. "Ow!" she yelled. "Watch where you're going, idiot!"

Great. Headbutting one of Sarah's boobs definitely wasn't how I wanted to start the conversation. I drew in a quick breath, inhaling about a gallon of her vanilla perfume. "I'm so sorry!"

Troy roared out a laugh and stomped up next to me. "That was awesome! Hey, you should add that move in your next video!"

"Don't you have some classes you have to go fail?" Sarah hissed.

That tore the smile right off the toad's face. Sarah's blue eyes zeroed in on me over her perfect little nose. "Mind telling me what *that* was about?"

"I swear it was an accident. I just didn't see you there," I said, doing a quick wedgie-out-of-the-crack dance.

Black-Haired Barbie planted her hands on her hips. "What do you mean you didn't see us? How could you not *see* us?"

"Come on, Sarah, we're gonna be late," Red-Haired Barbie groaned.

"Wait!" I shoved my hands in my pockets to keep

them from shaking. "I was wondering if I could ask you something."

Sarah gave me a quick up-and-down look.

"I entered this scholarship contest Dance-Splosion is having and—"

"Stop," she said, throwing a hand out in front of her. "Aren't you on the football team? No, wait, you're that Tighty Whitey kid." She laughed, with her Barbie horde joining in with her.

My entire body deflated. So much for ninja-kicking the door to dance awesomeness down. "Both actually."

"Since when do you dance?"

"Me? Uh, since, like, forever. Or since I quit karate last year, anyway. I never got past the green belt."

"That explains all the kicks and punches, then."

"Yeah, I call it . . ." I shrank a little lower, like my body was trying to curl into a ball and roll away from the embarrassment. "Ninja freestyle."

"Cute." Sarah checked the neon-blue polish on her fingernails. "So, what did you want?"

"Like I said, that video was my audition for Dance-Splosion's summer scholarship contest. And I was wondering . . ." My voice trailed off like a song fading out at the end.

"We don't have all day, Tighty Whitey," Black-Haired Barbie spat.

Sarah glanced over her shoulder. "Oh my God, Kaylee,

would you shut up?" She snapped her head back toward me, whacking the girls behind her with her fluffy blond ponytail. A smile spread over her glossy lips. "Let me guess. You want me to help you."

"Please! I'll work my butt off, I promise. I really need this, Sarah."

"Do you still dance with Kassie?"

My mind raced. I had a foot in the door, but one wrong word and that door could slam shut and crush it. I decided to play it safe. "Um, why?" Nothing safer than playing dumb.

"Well, if you are, I'm just wondering why you'd go behind her back and ask for my help."

Playing dumb had worked once. So I tried it again. "Um, I don't know?"

Sarah narrowed her eyes at me. Probably wondering why my IQ had suddenly dropped fifty points. "Sorry, Tighty Whitey. Competition season's still going on. I don't have time to babysit."

She walked off, her Barbie army trailing behind her. The door hadn't just slammed on my foot. It had cut off both legs and every chance I had at getting any better.

But then something happened. The dance gods reared back and tossed down a lightning bolt of brilliance. A heavenly Hail Mary pass of Second Chancery.

"Well, maybe Kassie will change her mind and help me, since she sent in a video, too."

Sarah spun around. "What did you just say?"

"Oh, I said Kassie sent in a video, too. She's been thinking about getting back into Dance-Splosion. Maybe she'll help me out."

"You're lying. She wouldn't do that."

I pulled out my phone. "Wanna call her and ask?"

For what seemed like forever, Sarah just stood there, freezing me in place with her Ice Queen stare of death. Red-Haired Barbie leaned over and whispered something in Sarah's ear. Her face lit up. I almost expected to see a little cartoon lightbulb pop up over her head.

"Fine. I'll help."

My heart skipped a beat, sending a wave of first-drop roller coaster excitement into my stomach. "Seriously?"

"We'll practice every Monday. Four o'clock in the gym. Don't be late." Sarah stomped off down the hall, the strutty hip-swinging gone from her step. She stopped and looked back over her shoulder. "Oh, and Tighty Whitey? Do yourself a favor and drop the wannabe dancers. The less of your bad dancing I have to fix, the better."

"Yeah, these look like a really fast pair."

Dad pulled the box of cleats down off the shelf. "Here, try these on. They're a half size bigger. You'll need some growing room."

"They look like all the others," I said. And they did. We'd been cleats shopping for an hour and I'd given up trying to convince him to get me jeans. Every one of my toes curled up at the thought of having to shove my feet into another pair of the stiff shoes. "Dad, I really don't want to play anymore."

"Son, we've talked about this. You committed yourself to the team. It wouldn't be fair to them."

"I don't even play! Like, ever!"

"So you're saying you're only important if you're out there on that field?"

"Uh, yeah. I'm not doing any good taking up space on the bench."

Dad crossed his arms. Which was a really bad sign. It meant he was three seconds away from saying something he thought was wise. "You remember Aunt Brenda, don't you?"

There it was. I nodded.

"For a while she was in the Army Reserves. She signed up right after she graduated high school. Went through all kinds of training, but she never did get called to active duty." Dad sat down next to me and took one of the cleats out of my hands. "Was she not important?"

"Yes. She was. But I'm talking about football, Dad. I really wanna focus on my dancing this year. The Dizzee Freekz need me more than the Sunnydale Sharks do."

"Dizzy Freaks?"

"Yeah, we, um—we named our dance crew the Dizzee Freekz. With a Z."

He shook his head like I'd told him we named ourselves the Fart Blossoms. "Karate, football—every team's got to have its support players. All this quitting worries me, Dillon."

"Seriously, Dad, you're making it sound like I'm about to drop out of school or something. It's just football. Plus, I'm twelve. Aren't I supposed to be quitting things, trying to figure out what I like and stuff?"

He stood and walked over to a wall of shoe boxes, staring at them for a while. When he turned to me, he was smiling. "Remember when you were five and you made Austin wrap you up in the garden hose?"

"Ugh." I let my head fall back against the shelf behind me. But I was smiling, too.

"From head to toe. And you told him to pull the end to see if you'd spin like a top. You went, 'One, two, three, pull!' and jumped and you just—" Now he was laughing. Hard. Which got me laughing. Hard. He held his forearm up and let it fall. Just like I did.

"That's not funny," I said, tears forming in my eyes from giggling so much.

"I probably should've stopped you, but—"

"You saw it? I thought you were in the house or something!"

He shook his head. "Garage. I think I just wanted to see if it would really work."

I wadded up a piece of tissue paper from the shoe box and threw it at him. But I didn't blame him. I probably would've, too.

Dad took a deep breath. "I guess what I'm saying is— you're right. About trying new things."

My face froze in whatever half laugh, half scowl it was in. "Seriously?"

"As long as you can promise me you'll actually stick with the dancing, then I guess I'm okay with it."

I waited for him to point at me and say, *Ha, you should see your face—of course you're sticking with football, be-*

cause football is LIFE! He didn't, though. He just put the cleat back into the shoe box.

"Ready to go?" he asked.

I nodded. Before he could turn to leave, I flung my arms around him. "Thank you."

He patted my back. "You're welcome, kiddo. But you're still not getting those baggy jeans."

I laughed. I could live with that.

On the way to Kassie's house, I texted everyone the good news. When I got there, I ran upstairs to the room we'd named the Dance Cave.

Carson and Austin were hovering over Kassie's laptop like they'd just discovered a lost episode of *America's Best Dance Crew*.

"Dillon, you have to see this!" Carson pulled me over to the computer. "The mall's opening a new Smoothie-topia in three weeks."

"And they're celebrating their grand opening with a dance-off. A real dance competition!" Kassie said.

I read the information on the site. Registration was only twenty dollars. No age divisions. No categories. "This is so cool! Are we gonna enter?"

"Are you serious?" Kassie said. "Of course we are!"

Austin held up his camera like he filming us. "I could record it and edit it together with the other routines like a real music video."

"Yeah, I'm in! This could be amazeballs!" Suddenly,

it hit me. I took a step back, remembering my conversation with Sarah. "Wait a sec—no, this is bad. This is like the total opposite of amazeballs."

"What's wrong?" Kassie asked.

"I, um, sort of forgot to mention something. About Sarah."

"Oh, you mean besides you telling her I wanted to rejoin the studio?" Kassie cocked her hip out to the side. "Not cool, Dillon."

"Hey, it got her attention, didn't it? Anyway, she sort of wants me to quit the crew."

"See, I told you this was a bad idea!" Austin said.

"I'm not quitting, Austin. I just have to let her *think* I have. If she finds out I'm still dancing with you all, she may decide to dump me."

Carson threw his arms out to the side. "Perfect. How about I just grab my invisibility cloak. Now, where'd I put it?"

Kassie clapped her hands together. "Masks! We could wear masks! We could be like Sunnydale's version of the Jabbawockeez."

It wasn't a bad idea.

Jabbawockeez dancers were famous for wearing their masks and keeping their identities secret.

"I have tons of masks we could use," Carson said. "Halloween's my jam, guys."

"All right. I say we give it a shot," Kassie said.

"Hey, what if we put this one on our channel?"

"Ooh, good idea!"

"Our channel?" I repeated.

"Yeah, Austin made us a YouTube channel," Kassie said. "We're going to get some people to subscribe. Get our dance out there. Maybe end up on *Ellen*."

"Oh my gosh, if I got to dance with Ellen, I'd die," Carson said.

My heart did a dive roll in my chest. "Guys, we can't."

"Dude, come on," Austin said. "Music video! I can make it look awesome, I swear." He stuck his hands under his chin like he was about to beg.

"I know you can, Austin, but we don't have any masks yet. Are we forgetting about Sarah?"

"Already on it." Kassie ran out of the room, her footsteps fading away into soft thuds. When I turned back to Carson, he was grinning at me.

"What?" I asked.

"Oh, nothing. It's just cute, you thinking you're being all secretive."

"Secretive about what? I already told you guys about the video."

"Not that. Duh. I'm talking about Kassie. I think you need to tell her."

"Tell her what?"

"That you like her. Like, *really* like her. You two would make a cute couple."

On the blush scale, my face instantly went nuclear red. "I—I don't like Kassie. Not like that. I mean, yeah, she's great and nice and all. And an amazing dancer." I stopped myself before I mentioned how she had amazing eyes. Or how she'd twirl this one stray piece of hair around her finger when she got nervous.

Carson grinned and mimed locking the corner of his mouth. I turned toward Austin, hoping he'd say something to help me, but he was busy laughing into his hand.

Kassie walked back in and tossed each of us a wad of black fabric. "We'll use these until Carson can get us some better masks."

I knelt down, pretending to tie my shoes so she wouldn't see the pink that still had to be covering my cheeks.

"*Panty hose?*" Carson yelped. "I'm not wearing an old pair of your mom's underwear on my head!"

"They're brand-new. And panty hose aren't underwear. They're like really thin tights."

Great. My first pair of tights.

And I got to wear them on my face.

"Do I get a pair?" Austin asked.

"You'll be behind the camera the whole time," Kassie said, shoving the panty hose over Carson's head.

"Trust me, you don't want any," Carson said as Kassie wrapped the panty hose legs around his mouth.

"It's not bad. You can't tell they're panties," I said.

"Panty *hose*," Kassie corrected me. She masked herself and we stood there for a second looking at each other before we burst into laughter.

"I'm totally making a blooper reel of this," Austin said, giggling.

"Okay, let's get into our positions," Kassie said, thumbing through the songs on her phone. "We'll run through it once like we practiced. See how they work."

She walked back to her spot as our song forced its way through the phone's tiny speakers.

Kassie took a step forward and flew into a spin.

Even with her face covered in black hose, her eyes blazed with an intensity that could melt a hole through lead. The way her arms whipped around as she turned made her look like a warrior princess slashing down evil orcs and demons with her battle-like dance moves.

Then the music stopped.

"Um, dude?" Austin said, holding Kassie's phone. "That was your cue."

"What?" I said, blinking fast. "Oh. Sorry. Can we start over? I was just, um, adjusting my panties."

"*Hose*. They're panty *hose*." Kassie grabbed her phone.

I forced my mind into dance mode. The music started up again and Kassie spun. It looked amazing. Not that I noticed.

She planted her feet. The music swelled. My turn to tell the story.

I took a deep breath and launched myself into the air.

I pulled my arms around me and twisted my body into a spin kick. As fast as my foot flung by, I was surprised I didn't hear a whip-crack sound. As soon as I landed, I dropped to the ground with one leg stretched behind me and one hand on the ground for support.

Kassie floated around the floor for a few seconds. I made my way behind her. I reached to the right and she reached left—the one part of the choreography I could nail. Then we both hopped back just as Carson jumped in with a toe touch that would've ripped a normal person's body completely in half (not to mention their jeans).

Carson and I each grabbed one of Kassie's hands. She pulled us toward each other. I slid under and Carson jumped over, his body almost parallel to the ground.

What I would've given to be able to do a move like that.

The music hiccupped and everyone froze.

Again, nailed it.

A funky dubstep groove crept up and Kassie dropped to her knees. The *womp womp* pulsed through the speakers and Kassie pushed herself forward and up to her feet. Just as the first electronic downbeat hit, Kassie was captured. Carson, the alien overlord, had turned her into a mechanical version of herself that moved in fast, popping moves, bending and twitching her body like she was part cyborg.

It was up to me, the samurai warrior, to save her. Carson whipped his arms through the air like they were made of ribbon. I jumped toward him and let loose a barrage of jumps and turns, swinging my arms this way and that, a kick here and an imaginary sword thrust there.

Carson's spin caught my eye. Without thinking, I threw one leg across my body and spun on one foot.

Once.

Twice.

Three times.

Four times!

When I stopped, the room didn't. I stumbled, falling right into a bookshelf behind me and bringing down Kassie's entire library on top of my head.

"Cut!" Austin yelled.

The gigantic novel covering my eyes was pulled off me. Kassie smiled down, worry filling her eyes. "Are you hurt?"

"Physically? No."

She laughed and helped Carson pull me to my feet. "One day we're going to find a spot for that shelf where it doesn't get in your way."

"Look at it this way," Carson said. "The stage at the mall probably won't have anything he can crash into."

"You're hilarious," I said.

Kassie peeled the cloth away from my eyes. "We

can take a break if you want to." Her voice was soft. Practically a whisper. There wasn't a bit of judginess in it, either. Of course, there never was.

"Nah." I tightened the hose around my head. "Let's run it again."

After that last run-through, it wasn't like I could get any worse.

6

▲▲▲▲▲▲▲▲▲

You can't handle the AWESOME!

Austin had made a banner at the top of our Dizzee Freekz YouTube channel with that on it. As soon as we picked our official masks, Kassie wanted to add a crew photo.

On Monday, I could barely eat my breakfast. I was having my first practice with Sarah and a knot was taking up all the room in my stomach.

When I walked into the cafeteria at lunchtime, Kassie was already there, sitting at our table.

"Hey!" I said, sitting down across from her.

"'Sup, fellow Dizzee Freek?"

A smile stretched across my face. "I can't stop thinking about our competition."

"I know, right? It's going to be so cool!"

We sat there for a second just grinning at each other. My face suddenly felt like it was about to burst into flames. And then an image of Carson locking his mouth popped into my head. I gave my chocolate milk a good shake and pushed the picture away. "Hey, um, mind if I ask you something?"

"Go ahead."

"I was thinking about our plan over the weekend and it got me wondering." I cleared my throat. "The whole studios-are-for-sellouts rule—is that all because of what happened with Sarah?"

Her mouth did this cute sideways pucker like she was deep in thought. "Pretty much. When I started dancing, I was just doing the moves that fit. Like you do. But the longer I was at Dance-Splosion, the more my teachers kept trying to change everything. Like they knew how my body was supposed to move to the music. Which is why I never got any solos at the competitions."

"So you didn't like them bossing you around?"

"No. I mean, yeah, that's part of it. But it's more like—you know how sometimes when we all watch a movie together, Austin laughs at certain parts and Carson laughs at others?"

I nodded.

"It'd be like if Carson got mad at us for not laughing at the things he thought were funny."

"He always does that."

"True. But imagine if he *made* us laugh at those parts because he thought that was the right thing to do. It'd kind of ruin the movie, right?"

"Yeah. I guess it would."

"Studios do that with dancing. Every teacher I had was the same. They'd force steps into my dance because they thought they were the right ones. And after a while, it started to ruin dancing for me."

I took a bite of my hamburger, thinking about what she'd said. "So they gave away your solo just because you weren't following the rules. That stinks."

Kassie picked up a French fry and stared at it. "Yeah. It does."

"And it stinks even more than Sarah agreed to take it. I'm starting to see what Carson was saying."

"No. I mean, yeah, Sarah took it and I'll never forgive her for it. But it's the studios that're the enemy. No matter who I told, they didn't care. All they wanted was another win." Her eyes drifted up to mine. "People deserve to know the truth about that place."

I needed to say something epic. Something the hero in a movie would say. But all I managed was a quick gulp of milk that nearly spewed out my nose when it went down the wrong pipe.

"Whoa, easy there, Dillon." Carson gave me a slap on the back and sat down. Austin plopped into the seat beside me.

"Sorry." I wiped my chin and immediately wished I

wasn't sitting right across from Kassie, gagging on my drink.

Austin slammed his hand on the table, making me jump in my seat. Thankfully, I'd already set my drink down. "Hey, I almost forgot. I had a thought."

"Congratulations," Carson said.

"Shut up. Anyway, what I was thinking was that we should get some business cards made and hand them out around school and stuff."

"No!" I said, my voice raspy from the coughing. "Not school. What if Sarah sees it?"

"But—" Austin groaned and tore open the plastic wrapper on his fork. "So much for getting people to subscribe."

"No, Austin, it's a really good idea," Kassie said. "Maybe not at school, but we could hand them out everywhere else."

He nodded, but not before giving me one quick scowly look. I was about to take another drink of my milk when the smell of vanilla tickled my nose. I perked up, recognizing the scent. Perfume.

"Well, look who it is," Sarah said, standing at the end of our table. Kassie's face went icy cold. It was like a blanket of tension had dropped right on the table. And it was seriously heavy.

"I didn't think you were allowed to be this close to food, Sarah," Carson said.

"I'm taking that as a compliment for how some of us didn't get fat over the summer," Sarah said coolly.

Carson waved away her comment.

"What do you want?" Kassie hissed.

"From Little Miss Dance Rebel? Nothing. But I think I need to have a talk with one of your friends." She swung her gaze toward me.

"I—I was, um, just—"

"You can have him," Kassie said. "He was just telling us he can't dance with us anymore."

I said a quick *Thank you, God, for letting Kassie be smarter than me* prayer.

"Yeah. So much for loyalty, I guess," Carson added, playing along.

Austin had his face practically buried in his tray, shoving fries in his mouth.

"Good," Sarah said. "Now, let's go. It's time you started eating with the team like the rest of the players." She walked off and our end of the table let out a collective sigh of relief.

Kassie laughed. "Okay, that was, like, really close."

Carson leaned over his tray, grinning. "You're going to be eating with DeMarcus Jones! I'm not gonna lie, Dillon, I'm sort of jealous right now."

"Well, not for long," I said. "Today's the day I hand in my jockstrap."

Carson's smile disappeared. "Gross."

I looked at Austin. "Hey, you all right?"

"I'm fine. Go have lunch with your new fake friends."

I waited for him to say something else, but he didn't. "Okay. Well, wish me luck, I guess." I picked up my tray and made my way to the football table. The only empty seat was next to Troy. Wonderful.

Sarah had parked herself with the Barbies on one side of her and DeMarcus on the other. Since he was the first-string quarterback, I didn't know much about him. Except that he had a cannon for an arm and he looked like Jaden Smith.

Sarah dipped one of her fries in his ketchup. "You know, Dillon, for a second I thought you might have been lying to me."

"No, I swear I wasn't. I was breaking up with them, like Kassie said."

"Ha! Tighty Whitey divorced his dance dorks," Troy said, stealing the mustard packets off my tray.

DeMarcus looked over my head toward my old table. Then at Sarah. Then at me. "I thought you guys were some sort of team or something."

I shrugged. "Not anymore."

"Why'd you quit?"

"Because Sarah told him to," Red-Haired Barbie said.

DeMarcus sighed, shaking his head. "Do you enjoy bossing everyone around?" he asked Sarah.

"I'm not bossing him around. I'm helping him. Dillon's

trying to win a Dance-Splosion scholarship. I'm helping his image."

She bumped DeMarcus with her shoulder like she was being all playful. But his jaw tensed up like something she'd said made him nervous.

Sarah rolled her eyes. "Oh, stop. Look, it doesn't take a genius to figure out they're bad for his image. Especially since his image already needs a miracle."

"Tighty Whitey! Tighty Whitey!" Troy chanted with a spaghetti noodle hanging from his mouth.

"Shut up, Troy," DeMarcus said.

"Why? Who cares what I call him?"

"I do. He's still a part of the team."

"Yeah, about that," I said. "I'm actually dropping out. Of football, I mean."

The color drained from Sarah's face. "What? I didn't tell you to do that."

"Yeah, I know. I figured it was time, since I never really get to play. Plus now I'll get to work even harder on my dance moves."

"You can't quit!"

"Um, pretty sure I can. People do it all the—"

"No, I mean I won't let you. You completely destroyed your reputation with that video, Dillon. Trust me, even my dropping your name at the studio won't erase your underwear from people's minds. We have to think about your resumé."

"Resumé? I can't get a job, I'm only twelve."

"I know that, stupid. I'm talking about your extra-curricular resumé."

"Oh," I said, feeling relieved. "Well, why can't I do something besides football?"

"Yeah, that's a great idea!" she said sarcastically. "You could join the drama club. Or maybe even the choir. Oh, I know, you could join the art club."

Black-Haired Barbie leaned forward, her face scrunched up in confusion. "Uh, we don't have any of those, Sarah."

"Exactly," she said. "Which is why you're sticking with football."

"But I already told my dad I was gonna quit!"

"Then un-tell him. Those judges want someone who's serious. Someone who's going to look as good on paper as they do on the floor. And trust me, they'll eat up the athlete-turned-dancer angle."

"Whatcha got against football, Tighty Whitey?" Troy growled.

"Nothing. I just don't want to play it anymore."

"It's not like you're ever on the field," Sarah said. "Just show up and sit on the bench like you always do. I'll take the pictures. Hopefully we can get enough of you not looking like a complete dork during prac-tice. With my help, you may actually have a chance at that scholarship."

"This isn't fair. Like, at all," I said.

"Listen," Sarah hissed. "Dance-Splosion is an elite academy. Dancers all over the country apply to our school and never get accepted. Which means we're seriously picky about who we let in. I'm not a miracle worker, okay? If you want to even stand a chance at that scholarship, then you need to meet me halfway. Got it?"

I was stuck in a maze and the walls were slowly closing in. But I couldn't turn back. Not when everything I wanted was ahead of me. "Fine," I said. It came out more sigh than actual word.

"Perfect."

"Can I go back to my table?"

Sarah shook her head. "I already told you. You're a football player. You need to eat with the team."

DeMarcus leaned close to Sarah and whispered, "Let him eat where he wants to."

"He *is* eating where he wants to. Isn't that right, Dillon?"

My eyes bounced around the table, landing on face after face. If smiles could be animals, the one that slithered across Sarah's mouth would be the world's most venomous snake.

And I was the little mouse for lunch.

▲▲▲▲▲▲▲▲▲

Kassie and Carson were waiting for me outside after the 3:30 bell.

"Austin already leave?" I asked, tossing my backpack down against the wall.

Carson shook his head. "I saw him sitting outside the nurse's office. He didn't look too good."

"Well, at least I'm not the only one with a sucky day." I slid down the wall beside my backpack.

"What happened?" Kassie asked, kicking my foot.

"Sarah's making me stick with football. She said my reputation needed it."

Carson barked out a loud "Ha!" then added, "You know you don't have to do that."

"Yeah, right."

"He's right, Dillon." Kassie squatted down beside me. "If this whole thing's too much, just say so."

"Um, I was just talking about football," Carson said. "I wasn't saying he needed to forget the whole plan."

Kassie breathed in slowly, then said, "I'll back you up no matter what you choose."

When Kassie had first brought up the plan, it had scared me to death. But knowing I was going to look like a hero to her for trying was enough to make me want to stick with it. Plus the whole getting-some-dance-help thing was really cool, too. "I'm still in."

"Sweet!" Kassie grabbed one of my shoelaces and yanked it loose. I rolled my eyes, but I couldn't help smiling. I liked to pretend that doing stuff like that was her way of flirting. She stood up and pulled a piece of notebook paper out of her pocket. "Now tell me what you think of this business card design."

Our crew logo. It looked perfect. Big purple block letters for *Dizzee* with *Freekz* underneath it in dark, jagged black lines. Behind the words was a big yellow star.

"That's awesome!" I said. "How'd you get so good at drawing? I can't even draw a stick figure."

"Aww, I like your stick figures."

A goofy-sounding laugh popped out of my mouth and I covered it up with a cough. Carson turned his head like he was trying to hide his smile.

"Okay, so since our plan's still on, I'm going to see if

we can preorder tickets to the Heartland Dance Challenge," Kassie said.

"Yes! There's no way I'm going to miss the look on Sarah's face. She'll be all like—" Carson's face twisted up into this fake surprised look. He marched around me and Kassie, pretending to bump into people like he was in the middle of the world's most awkward escape mission. It was hilarious. Several other students stopped to watch him, giggling as he acted like he kept twisting an ankle while he walked.

All of a sudden he stopped, looking at the line of vehicles in the car rider line. "Okay, never mind. I know exactly how embarrassed she'll be."

It wasn't hard to figure out what he was talking about. Carson's mom and dad were the world's most intense dance parents. They had their car decked out in every dance-themed bumper sticker they could find. They'd even had some made up with his face on them. It drove Carson insane.

"Excuse me while I run away forever."

"Later," I said, trying not to laugh. I turned to Kassie. "I'll see you tomorrow. If I survive Sarah."

Sarah was already waiting in the gym, decked out in a T-shirt and black tights. I slapped the pinch of jealousy away and walked over to her.

"You're not practicing in that."

I glanced down at my jeans. "What else am I supposed to practice in?"

"Anything but jeans. We both know your dancing and jeans don't mix."

"Well, it's either this or my underwear. And the world's seen enough of that."

"Then put on your football pants. If you're going to dance for real, then you need to dress the part."

"Yeah, because nothing says dance like football pants."

Sarah nearly tore my head off with the scowl on her face.

"Fine. I'll change." I went to the locker room and opened my locker. My pants were right where I'd left them last year. Shoved in the back corner.

I held them up. They looked almost like real dance tights. I couldn't help but smile. That was until I turned them over and remembered mine had a massive dirt stain running down the backside. My second pair of tights and they had a skid mark as long as my arm. But at least I didn't have to wear them on my head.

I got changed and came out trying to pull my T-shirt down as low as it could go. After a few minutes of stretching, I was already sweating. Normally I just ran in place for a few seconds.

"Okay," Sarah finally said. "Feet in first position."

"Huh?"

"First pos— Oh good grief. Put your feet like this." Sarah slid her heels together. "The judges are going to want to see control. So none of your punching and kicking, okay?"

I was surprised it stung as bad as it did. Punching and kicking was the only thing I was good at. But I was there to learn the new stuff. The real dance moves.

"We'll be creating a new routine for you. From scratch. But before I can do that, I'll need to see what you can do. Let's see your *plié*." She pronounced it "plee-ay."

If that meant "stare blankly," I was nailing it. But apparently it didn't. It meant "squat down as far as you can without falling over." Then she made me try a *développé* (she pronounced it "dev-low-*pay*"), which was basically a side kick. Each time I did one, she'd push my knee down or shove my toes forward. I tried my left leg, but it was less flexible than the right. But after about the twentieth time, I was starting to get it.

My body was doing actual dance moves.

A jolt of excitement rocketed through me.

"Why are you smiling like that?" Sarah asked.

"Because . . . this is pretty awesome. I never thought I'd be doing moves like this."

"Well, calm down. Because you're, like, really bad. Especially your feet."

"Gee. Thanks." I pulled the bunch of spandex out of my crack. My feet pointed just fine when I wasn't dancing, but every time I moved they'd bend or "sickle." Whatever that meant.

"Look," she said. "You're not pushing your toes forward. Imagine your heel in front of them. Like this."

Sarah leaned forward while her left leg floated up behind her. Her arms flowed out to the side like tiny waves. The move was so simple. So effortless. So gorgeous. I sat down, never taking my eyes off her. I'd never actually seen Sarah Middleton dance. And in that pose, she was something different. It was like every bit of her angry snark faded away. Even her face softened. I was seeing a hidden person underneath the layer of snobbery she usually wore.

And then she lowered her leg and it all vanished.

POOF!

"I don't know why you can't do it. Didn't Kassie or Carson see all of your mistakes?"

I shrugged. "They're more about getting out there and having fun, I guess. If I couldn't do a move, we'd just sort of scrap it."

"Dance is about technique, not having fun. So if I say do a move, you do it. There is no move-scrapping in dance."

"But what if it won't fit?"

"'Won't fit'? What does that even mean?"

"Kassie always says—I mean *said*—that *I'm* the one who has to find the moves to fit *me*. She said dance is about expression, and if there's a move that doesn't help you tell a story and express yourself, then it doesn't belong."

Sarah's eyes dropped to the floor for a second like

something I'd said had stung her. She looked back at me, her face wrenched up in disapproval. "Well—that's just stupid. If you expect to make it to the top three, then you need to forget everything Kassie ever told you about dance. Especially since she's your competition now."

There was no way Kassie could've been *that* wrong. She was the best dancer I'd ever seen.

"Now get up. Let's try something easy. The walk."

Walking? I was pretty sure I had that down. But not how she showed me. Apparently, in the dance world, walking meant swinging your feet out in front of you like your legs were frozen stiff.

I did my best to copy her moves. Each time, I heard Kassie's voice in my head.

Copying someone will just strangle all your creativity.

But then why did it feel so good to do it? All the best dancers did the same moves.

"Toes, toes, *toes!*" Sarah yelled. "All you're doing is walking, so point your toes!"

I reset. Heels together. Step. Toes forward. Heel in front. Step. Toes forward. Heel in front. After a few more, I found that clenching my butt helped. Like I'd just gotten a wedgie from Troy.

"Better," Sarah said. "Sort of."

I jumped, punching the air to celebrate. I couldn't be sure, but I thought Sarah might've smiled. If she did, it was quick. "Back to first. Let's try something else. I'm not even going to pretend you can do an arabesque, so we'll start with what the first years do. A *retiré*." She pronounced it "reh-tee-*ray*." She pulled her left foot up, toe pointed, letting it touch her right knee. She stood there like a statue and nodded to me.

Piece of cake. I pulled my foot up, forcing my toes back toward my heel like she'd taught me, and touched my knee. I had to hold my arms out for balance, and I wiggled a little bit, but I was totally—

"GAH!"

It was like my leg got shut in a car door. On a cramp scale from one to ten, my calf was at a thirty. I grabbed my leg and fell straight back, yelling the entire way. I landed on my butt as the knot worked its way deeper into my muscle. "I think it's getting worse!" I cried, and rolled on my back with my foot in the air.

I looked up at Sarah. My calf was collapsing into a black hole underneath my skin and she was laughing. I rolled back into a sitting position, still holding my foot as close to my chest as I could.

"It's not funny! This seriously hurts!"

"I know." She leaned down and forced my leg out straight. "I've just never seen someone get that freaked out over a cramp." She put her hands on my foot and pushed it back, stretching my calf. Some of the pain instantly disappeared. I let out a sigh of relief, watching her work her magic. After a few more seconds of her pushing my toes back and forth, she got up and crossed her arms. "Better?"

I worked my leg around a little. "Yeah. Thanks." I stood up, hopping on each leg to test it out.

"Good," Sarah said. "Then back to first position."

Whatever bit of *nice* or *pleasant* I thought I'd heard in her voice before was gone. Business-mode Sarah was in the house.

"I hope you're not scared of pain. Because if you're going to be a dancer—" Sarah took a deep breath and straightened her back. "There's going to be a lot of it."

Sarah wasn't lying.

My butt cheeks felt like they had a pair of ninja stars lodged in them from all the pliés. But even as bad as they hurt, I couldn't stop smiling. Because the throbbing was from the technique. Sarah told me if I was doing it right, I'd be sore. And I was definitely sore.

The only bad thing was that I had to learn it all from her. She yelled more than anyone I'd ever known. I got home with my head feeling like Troy had used it for a seat cushion.

And telling my parents I'd changed my mind about quitting football didn't help.

"I had a feeling you would," Dad said. "I remember

how exciting it was to get out there on the field. Nothing beats the smell of a football field on game day."

"Yeah. Nothing beats that sweaty-body-odor stench." I opened the fridge to get some orange juice.

"Didn't you say you were going to concentrate more on your dancing?" Mom asked me, staring at her laptop the entire time. "I thought you had that scholarship thing you were practicing for."

I shrugged. "I guess I can do both." Not like I had much of a choice, really. If I backed out of Kassie's plan now, I'd be giving up a ton of free dance lessons with Sarah.

But at least I finally got to dance in something besides jeans. I went to my room and practiced pliés and retirés and développés until my legs were about to fall off. I kept my football pants on the whole time. They made awesome tights. Those suckers were made out of space-age stretchy fabric and had two layers to protect any rear end from exposure, no matter how beefy.

Of course, the poop-brown stain running down the back wouldn't come out. No matter how many times Mom washed them.

At least the other football players didn't seem to care. When the team met after school the next day for the first practice of the season, everyone huddled in their usual groups. First string all together, talking and laughing. Second string doing the same thing.

And the blue team. My team. We just sort of stood around, looking at each other like we weren't really sure why we were even there.

"All right, men," Coach Bear said, waving us into one big group. He crossed his arms. They were so hairy it made his gut look like it had a unibrow. He dragged one hand down his mustache and sighed. "Thursday's our first game. Pine Ridge Middle."

Coach Donnelly nodded. "Gotta watch their back-field." He was basically a miniature version of Coach Bear.

"Yep. We're five-and-oh against 'em but that don't mean we ain't gonna go out there and play like we're oh-and-five, right?"

The team grunted out a round of cheers.

Coach Bear pulled his baseball cap down. I wasn't sure how he ever saw with it covering ninety percent of his eyes. "That's what I wanna hear! We're gonna go un-defeated, boys. I ain't gonna accept a loss. Not with the offense we got this year."

More cheers. Grunts.

"You know my favorite saying. *Second place is the first loser.* We gonna come in second Thursday?"

After a loud round of *NOs*, we took off for our warm-up jog.

Football practices would be so much better if they were like all the training montages I'd seen in the *Step Up* movies. The ones where the music starts and the hero gets a determined look on his face while he dances in front of the mirror, messes up, wipes the sweat off his face, and keeps going.

But they're not.

Like . . . at all.

They're more like getting chased by a whistle-blowing pit bull while you run through a trail of old tires and jump over cones with trip wires strung between them. Last year I almost passed out during our first few practices. I wasn't used to all the running and jumping.

This year was different. My body stayed on the edge of exhausted all the time, but I kept going. Even Coach Bear noticed me a couple of times.

I won't lie. It felt great.

I even got a "Not bad, Parker, now see if you can run like that with a ball in your hands" from him. He put me in on a play while Bobby Fleagle, the first-string running back, was getting some water. DeMarcus glanced back at me, giving me a *good job* nod.

My body buzzed with excitement. It made me want to push even harder. So I did. DeMarcus called, "Hike!" and rammed the ball into my stomach. I took off, remembering the way Bobby had gone the last few times he ran the play.

There had to be a trail of fire behind me, because I was a rocket and I wasn't about to stop.

Except I did. I didn't see who it was, but a pair of hands landed on my shoulders and shoved me over the sidelines. Our first practices were always padless, so we weren't allowed to tackle. But apparently throwing someone halfway to China was okay.

Thankfully, I didn't black out. However, I did land on my shoulder so hard the only sound I could make was a humming noise that sounded like a stray cat pushing out a litter of kittens.

The thud of footsteps filled my ears. My team-mates' heads popped into view one by one. The coaches shoved their way through the crowd. For a while nobody said anything. Which made it even worse. Like they were watching a cockroach on its back wiggling its way right side up. It was humiliating. My face felt red-hot and ten sizes bigger than usual. My hands were all sweaty, sliding over the bumpy covering of the—

The football! I yanked my head off the ground and looked at my hands. Yeah, I might've been tossed out of bounds by the Incredible Hulk, but I'd held on to the ball.

Coach Bear smiled. "Way to hustle, kid."

DeMarcus grabbed my hand and yanked me to my feet. "Nice run, Dillon." I did my best to play it cool, but trust me, inside, my stomach was dancing harder than the entire cast of *High School Musical.*

Even though my spine was probably broken. And my feet. Maybe Dad was right about needing new cleats after all.

At dinner, I almost collapsed into my plate of spaghetti. I barely even noticed the business talk they were throwing back and forth. The only thing that caught my attention was when Dad mentioned someone named Alan Scapelli and Mom got really quiet all of a sudden.

"Don't start on Alan again. He's a good guy. He's just got some weird business ideas," Dad said, probably reading the look on Mom's face.

"Like what?" I asked.

Mom pointed to Dad with her fork. "Your father thought it'd be a good idea to invest in a man who wants to buy up all the pennies in the southeast USA."

I almost choked on a noodle. "Seriously? Dad, that's just—weird."

"It's not weird. It's forward thinking," Dad said.

Mom mouthed, *No, weird.*

"Carol, stop. And it's not just pennies. It's any older coin."

"I still don't get it."

"Well, a lot of old coins are made from copper or silver. And they're worth more than their face value. So he's using the money I—*we*—invested and buying as many as he can. Then reselling them to companies that are looking for those types of metals."

I let it sit with me for a second. And then I shook my head and said, "Mom's right, that's weird."

"This is why you're my favorite child," she said, pretending to pinch my cheek.

Dad huffed. "Fine. But I've already got my *I told you so* speech ready when Alan comes through."

"Can't wait to hear that one." Mom smiled, but I could tell she was still irritated with him.

We spent the rest of dinner talking about anything we could except coins or money. I decided my feet could suffer through another season being cramped in a pair of slightly-too-small cleats.

By my first game on Thursday, I was having muscle pains in parts of my body I didn't even know could *get* sore. Like the back of the knee. How does that even work?

Luckily, all I had to do was hold the bench down with my butt. My knee-rears got to rest all the way through the first half of the game. I even untied my cleats so my toes could breathe.

During halftime, the speakers belted out the same Lynyrd Skynyrd songs they always played, and a bunch of people got up for bathroom breaks and concession stand visits.

I limped to the fence to talk to Kassie, Carson, and Austin.

"Hey, guys."

"Everyone, look! It's Dillon Parker," Kassie said, pretending to swoon.

"Think you'll actually get to do something this year besides keep the bench warm?" Austin asked.

"Um, ouch. Good to see you're feeling better," I said.

"Oh, uh, yeah. I'm fine." His eyes dropped to his feet.

"Was it the fries? Because those things gave me some serious gas."

"Dude, I said I'm fine. It was nothing." He smiled, but I could tell it was fake. There was something he wasn't telling me.

I decided halftime during my first game wasn't the best place to get into it. "Anyway, I've been getting to run plays every now and then during practice. Coach said I was pretty fast. Even got a slap on the butt from DeMarcus."

Carson's mouth fell open. "I hate you."

Me and Kassie laughed. I spotted Sarah snapping pictures of the crowd. "I better get back before Sarah sees me talking to you guys."

I waved at my parents on the top row and headed back toward the sidelines.

The second half of the game was like a replay of the

first. Our offense was way better than Pine Ridge's. We scored two more touchdowns and kept them from even getting near the end zone.

My favorite play was the one where DeMarcus would toss the ball to the fullback, Cody Ryans. He'd run one way like he was going to go right. But then hand it off to Bobby Fleagle, who'd take off in the opposite direction.

Classic fakeroo.

Before lunch on Friday, I texted Kassie an idea in the middle of math class.

Me: hey let's see if mrs. kellerman will let us eat in the room.
Kassie: y? u need help with homework?
Me: no we can all eat together. im tired of sitting with sarah.

There was a pause. I guessed Kassie was picking up the pieces of her mind that I'd just blown apart with my brilliant plan.

Kassie: i don't know. sounds risky. i think u should just eat with her 2 b safe.

Or not. So much for eating with my friends.

Me: fine. but if i starve 2 death it's bc troy won't stop eating all my food.

Kassie: LOL! well they can have u at lunch. but ur all mine on saturdays! :)

I shoved my phone back into my pocket before the teacher asked what I was growling at. Kassie's plan was pretty solid. And going undercover was actually pretty fun.

But there was only so much Sarah I could take.

▲▲▲▲▲▲▲▲▲

Our panty hose masks worked like a charm.

When we got to Carson's house on Saturday, the first thing we did was check our page views. None of the YouTube comments even hinted they knew who we were. We had a few like *OMG u look so stupid* and *GET A LIFE LOOSERS!* but we also had a couple of great ones. Like one that said we should add in some lifts.

"Obviously someone should lift me," Carson said. "I'm the lightest by far."

Kassie slapped his arm. "Watch it, stick boy."

I wrung my hands together. "I don't know. Don't you think it's a little late to be adding in stuff?"

"Not if we do something simple."

"No, it has to be something amazing." Carson clicked

on another link. "I'm telling you, we need to go full-on *Dirty Dancing* with this."

"Dillon's not strong enough to pick me up over his head like that!"

"Oh thanks, Kass."

"Fine, then, Mr. Football. Let's see if all that bench-pressing during practice is paying off." Kassie put my hands on her waist.

"Um, well, actually, all we do is run." My voice came out high-pitched and warbly.

"And booty slap each other," Carson said, smacking Austin's butt.

Austin tried to swat his hand away, but missed. "If you add in a lift now, it's gonna throw off the continuity."

"Party pooper." Carson crossed his arms. "Wait, what do you mean *continuity?*"

"For the music video. Editing this stuff's gonna be impossible if the dances are all different."

"Ugh! No one cares about the video, Austin." Carson immediately tensed up. "That came out wrong. I swear."

Austin's face stayed frozen, balled up in a wad of hurt.

Kassie stepped forward. "I think he just meant no one cares if the editing's not perfect."

For a few seconds, I was sure Austin was going to grab his camera and leave. I know he already felt like he didn't belong. He didn't need us to start telling him his only job didn't matter.

"But I think that stuff is important," I said. "The editing and continuation and stuff."

"Continuity," Austin said, correcting me.

"Yeah. That. So let's just wait on the lift. Make what we have, like, really perfect." The truth was, I sort of wanted to try a lift. But I wanted to keep Austin's feelings from getting hacked to pieces even more.

Kassie smiled. "Um, yeah. Dillon's right. We want the video to look as good as it can."

"See? Kassie knows what I'm trying to say. We don't want you to be upset," Carson said. He wrapped his arms around Austin and squeezed. "Especially since you have one serious ugly cry."

Austin laughed. "Get off me, you freak."

"I think you mean 'Dizzee Freek.' Oh, I almost forgot!" Carson let go of Austin and ran to a box on the shelf. "Our disguises."

We pulled the masks out, one by one.

Frankenstein. An old man smoking a cigar. Even a werewolf.

Carson already had his picked out. It was a fox. A perfect match to his personality.

Kassie found hers next. She pulled out one that didn't cover much more than her eyes and nose. It had feathers sprouting from the top. All the purple and black made her eyes look almost green.

"I don't care what you all say, I'm picking one." Austin shoved a few masks out of the way and pulled out a white mask that only covered half of his face. "Yes, this one! Dude," he said to Carson, "I can't believe you went as Jason from *Friday the 13th*. That's a little hard-core for you, isn't it?" He put it on under his glasses and ran back to the camera, looking through the eyepiece with his free eye.

"I don't have the heart to tell him that's a Phantom of the Opera mask," Carson mumbled.

I took a few out, hoping there'd be one left that'd at least cover my face without making me look like an idiot. Right when I was about to give up, I found it. "Whoa. Awesome." I held up a dark red ninja mask with yellow lines around the open part around the eyes. I turned it over in my hands. I was supposed to be moving away from all of the karate stuff in my dancing, but the mask was too perfect to pass up.

"Okay, let's put these bad boys on and see if we can get through the routine without breaking something," Kassie said.

"Oh, let me do something first." I grabbed my duffel bag and ran into the house. In less than two minutes, I made my way back to the garage with my football pants on.

Carson's jaw dropped. "You finally got some tights!"

"Not exactly," I said, putting on my mask. "Football pants. But they're not too bad."

"What about the jeans?" Kassie said.

"I can't dance in those. And these aren't tights, so all three of us are still wearing something different."

Kassie stared at them for what seemed like forever.

"Please?" I begged. "I'm gonna have to suffer through Sarah torturing me every Monday. The least you could do is let me wear them."

She sighed. "I guess it'll be okay, since Carson's tights are black and yours are white."

I jabbed a fist into the air and turned around to start stretching. Austin roared with laughter. "Hold on, Kassie, they're not *all* white!"

Great. I was so excited about wearing something besides jeans, I'd forgotten they hadn't seen the stain before. Until now it had always been covered by my football jersey, which was so big it hung down past my butt.

"Well, at least no one's gonna be calling you Tighty Whitey anymore. More like Tighty Brownie," Austin said.

Carson picked up a stray mask and threw it at him.

"Oh, I'm so glad you said that, Austin." Kassie glanced at me. "I mean not about the stain. About the nick- name. Because I was thinking it'd be good to come up with one in case Sarah hears about the dance-off."

Austin let out a loud groan. "Does everything we do have to be about tricking her? Why can't you all just dance and I can record it like we used to?"

"If you're about to tell us you have a crush on Sarah . . . ," Carson said, his eyes nearly popping out of his head.

"I'm not—I'm just saying it's getting sort of old."

"We're not doing this to trick her," Kassie said. "We're doing this so Dillon won't get caught. And, no, that's not the same thing."

"Fine," Austin said. "Then I call Jason."

"Jason's not a nickname," Carson said. "It has to be something catchy."

"Then I call Dr. Doom."

"Better. I'm going to be C-Note," Carson said, striking a pose. "Because these moves are rich, baby."

"Nice." Kassie pulled a note from her pocket. "I wrote down a few but the one I really like for me is Mystic."

She held out the paper, letting us see how she spelled it. *Misstik.* We all agreed it was perfect.

When it was my turn, all I could think of was, "Anything except Tighty Whitey. Or Brownie."

My mind wouldn't stop going through all the ways I'd embarrass myself at the dance-off. Falling off the stage. Breaking a bone while I tried to jump like Carson. Breaking someone else's bones while I tried to do a move like Kassie.

I wasn't new to competing. I'd had to spar with an opponent for every belt I'd earned in karate. But this was different.

This was at a *mall*.

Luckily, I made it through practice without breaking anything. Or getting a cramp.

The top of my head lifted open and the notes poured in. I forgot about all the junk I'd gotten myself into and concentrated on the music. I needed to let it all out.

I kicked, I jumped, I twirled imaginary nunchucks like I was the Teenage Mutant Ninja Turtle of Dance.

I even busted out some karate-style popping and locking, combining it with one of those cool arm waves breakdancers do. It looked terrible, I'm sure. But I forced the worry part of my brain into hibernation mode and kept on going.

When the music finally stopped, my heart was humming in my chest. Not because I was out of breath. But because the moves . . .

As awful as they were—as bent and nasty and crooked as everything probably was—

They fit me.

While the video uploaded, we worked on math homework in Carson's room. Or more precisely, three of us worked on math while Kassie tried to help everyone understand how we were supposed to use Horatio's number of steps taken to figure out Julia's number of steps.

Because apparently Julia couldn't count her own.

"This is pointless," Carson said, slamming his pencil down. "Why do we even need to know how many she took? She's walking down a hallway, not trying to find her way out of the Temple of Doom."

Austin tossed his mask up in the air and caught it. "I just wrote down fifty-three so it sounds like I used some sort of formula to figure it out."

"You guys are making this a lot harder than it should be," Kassie said. She leaned back against the wall and hit play on the video. Carson leaned over the edge of the bed to watch with her.

Austin started to scoot over beside her, but I grabbed his arm. "Hey, can I talk to you for a sec?" He sat back down. "Are we, like, okay?"

He shrugged. "I guess. Why?"

"It's just been weird. You seem like you've been mad at me."

He let out a long breath. "I'm not *mad*. Just—I guess I never thought you'd actually go through with all of this."

"I haven't gone through with anything yet."

"Yeah, but you will. And I know they keep saying Sarah and the studio are, like, really awful, but it still seems like a super jerky thing to do."

Sarah. Again. For a second I wondered if Carson was right. Maybe Austin did have a crush on her. I wouldn't blame him. She was definitely pretty.

"And part of me is worried that you *won't* go through with it and we'll never get to film our zombie movie. It's like no matter what happens, it kind of stinks."

"Don't worry, man," I said. "I'll never even make it

to the top three. Sarah won't ever know what we had planned and next summer we'll make the bloodiest zombie movie ever."

Austin stared at me for a second, then nodded. I gave him a friendly nudge to make sure he knew I was serious. He nudged back to let me know he did.

"Oh my gosh, I've got it!" Kassie yelled.

Austin and I ran over to where she was sitting. "What?"

"I have the perfect one." She had the screen paused where I was in the middle of a side kick. I looked awesome. Like I could be on the poster for *Last Ninja 3*.

"What are you talking about?" I asked.

"Your nickname." She grabbed my mask off the floor and held it in front of me. "You're the Kung Fu Kid."

10

▲▲▲▲▲▲▲▲▲

I karate-chopped my way all through the weekend.

I was the Kung Fu Kid.

And I was feeling better than I had in a long time. Things were finally getting back to normal.

Me and Austin texted back and forth, sending each other pictures we took using an app called Zombify Yourself. He sent me one of his dog, so I spent most of Sunday afternoon trying to get good candid photos of Mom and Dad. They probably would've just let me take one of them, but it was more fun to be sneaky about it.

On Monday, I was walking toward first period when DeMarcus nearly scared me to death.

"Hey, Dillon, wait up."

I spun around. "Me?"

It wasn't like there were a ton of Dillons at Sunnydale. I was just surprised he'd want to talk to me. Then surprise turned to worrying whether he was jealous that I'd been hanging around Sarah. Or maybe he knew about our plan. Fear finally took over. My armpits instantly went sweaty at the thought of the quarterback getting our offensive line to shove me into a locker.

"I promise she's just helping me with dance. That's all," I blurted out.

His face scrunched up like he was confused and then he laughed. "Oh, Sarah? No, I don't care about that."

"Oh. Okay." My pulse slowed to normal speed.

"It's about—" He grabbed my arm and led me over to the water fountain. "It's about that dance team thing you're on."

"I quit it. I swear."

"But you're still friends with them?"

I glanced around, trying to find Sarah. She must've sent him to pry the truth out of me. I chomped down on my bottom lip.

DeMarcus rolled his eyes. "Calm down, I'm not gonna go tell on you."

"Okay," I said, swallowing.

"Cool. So, they don't have, like, any weird rules, do they? Like ones about dating football players or something?"

I almost laughed. But before I could, it hit me. The tallest, most popular guy in school was asking about Kassie. Of course she didn't have any rules about who she could date, but I wasn't about to tell *him* that.

"But you're dating Sarah."

He shushed me quiet. "I know that. I'm just asking."

"Oh. Well, um, I—I think Kassie does have a rule about dating athletes." It was a lie, sure. But I was sort of desperate.

"Gotcha," he said. "So is that, like, a team rule? For everyone?"

"Well, she's the only girl." A tiny laugh sneaked past my lips. "So unless you wanna go out with Carson—"

"Hey!" DeMarcus took a step toward me. "I didn't say anything about him, did I?"

"No," I said, shrinking back. "I'm sorry." There I was, squished in between the water fountain and the wall while the entire school went by totally unaware that I was probably two seconds away from being turned into ground Dillon.

But DeMarcus never threw a punch. To be honest, he didn't even look mad. He just stared at the ground for a few seconds, rubbing his hands together.

"I didn't mean anything. I promise," I said.

"Huh? Oh, uh, just—just forget about it." Then he left. Leaving me wedged in the corner and completely confused.

After the last bell, I got changed into my dance gear (Sarah made me stop calling them football pants) and went to the gym. We ran through our stretches and I did a few extra foot rolls to make sure my calf wouldn't go all traitor on me.

"I hope you're ready to work today." Sarah pulled out her phone and started playing a soft stringy song with no lyrics. It sort of sounded like slow Christmas music. "Because you're learning your choreography."

"Are you serious?" I asked. "I'm dancing to this?"

"No. But you'll be dancing to something like it, I'm sure. When you make it to the top three—"

"You mean *if*."

"No, I mean *when*. We have to stay positive. Now, *when* you make it to the top three, you'll have to perform an improvised solo for the judges."

"Um—you do realize *improvised* means I make it up as I go, right?"

Sarah put a fist on one of her hips. "Um, you do realize you can't dance, right?" She went into first position. "Now, we'll focus on your strengths. Which you don't have a ton of. But your leaps aren't all terrible, so you're going to start out with a *sissonne*."

"A see-saw?"

"See-*sown*." She huffed and showed me how to do it. She hopped to the side and landed on her right foot.

I tried one of my own and was pretty sure I'd nailed it.

"Point your toes!" She smacked her hands together with each word. "And keep your right leg straight!"

Or maybe I didn't.

"Do it again. And please try not to look like a total spaz."

I did it again. And again. And about five hundred times more. Finally she let me go on to my next move. A step-step-spin combo.

I fanned my shirt, glancing around to make sure there was nothing close enough for me to run into.

"You remember how to step, at least?"

"Uh-huh." The stick-up-the-butt stiff-legged walk.

"Good. Now you'll take two of those and start with a single pirouette." She double-stepped and brought her right leg up to her left knee to start the spin.

"A retiré! I remember that from last week!"

Sarah spun once and her arms floated back down to her sides. "Now let's see you try it."

I attempted the move a few times. The first was beyond awful. The times after that weren't any better. The more I tried, the more worried I got. All the good feelings I'd felt after the first practice were gone, buried under the fear that there was just something wrong with me. Like maybe the dance chunk of my brain was broken or something.

"Don't shrug when you move. Try to make your neck longer," Sarah said, stretching hers out, looking like someone posing for the front cover of *Snob* magazine.

I tried to do the same thing.

"No, don't pull your shoulders down. Just relax."

So I did.

"You're slumping. Straighten your back."

I did that, too.

"You're tensing up. *Relax*."

I threw my hands in the air. "I *am* relaxing! I just can't do it."

"Yes, you can. Now come back and—"

"No, I can't! I guess I'm just not made to dance like that."

Sarah stopped the music. "Did you expect to learn it on the first try?"

I just stood there, my chest burning from breathing so hard.

"Look, Dillon, you're not going to win this thing if you give up as soon as it gets tough. Let's run it again."

"This is stupid! All you care about is rules and form and having body parts in just the right spot. It's starting to not even feel like dance anymore."

Sarah stomped toward me so fast I thought she might tackle me. "You want to know why I care about that stuff so much? It's because that's what separates the amateurs from the pros. That's what it takes to be the best, Dillon. It takes commitment. It takes drive. It takes doing whatever you have to do to make sure you come out as number one. Even if—" She took a deep breath. Almost like she didn't want to finish. But she did. "Even if it hurts more than you think you can handle."

We stood there in the world's most awkward silence for a long time. Then she ran her hand through her ponytail and looked at me. "Look, maybe I *have* been a little hard on you. But I promise it's for your own good."

"Yelling at me is for my own good? I hope you realize the more you break a lung screaming at me, the more I think maybe Kassie's right." I wiped the sweat off my brow. "Or was. When she hated studios, I mean."

"You can drop the act," Sarah said, rolling her eyes. "I know she didn't send in a video."

My chest tightened, forcing a sound out of my mouth. Somewhere between a grunt and the word *Huh?*

The *Then why are you helping me?* plastered across my face must've been obvious. "It doesn't matter why I'm helping you," Sarah said. "I have my reasons. Now reset."

She knew. And she was still keeping me around. A tiny prickle of worry inched across my skin. Something wasn't making sense.

Sarah smacked her hands together. "Come on, let's go."

"Not until you tell me why you're helping."

"Like I said. That's not important."

"It is to me! What if you're teaching me all kinds of stupid moves on purpose so I'll look bad when I win?"

Sarah smiled. "You said *when*. Good. And these moves are not stupid, by the way."

"How should I know?"

"Listen, Dillon. I've totally got the upper hand here. You want help? I'm giving it. I don't have to tell you why. If you don't like it, you can walk out. I don't care." She flipped her ponytail back over her shoulder. "So what's it going to be?"

I stood there for a few seconds, thinking. Really thinking. All the yelling and making fun of my dancing? And for some secret reason she wouldn't tell? I wasn't sure it was worth it. Not even a little.

So, yeah. I thought. Hard.

In the end, though, I walked back to the middle of the gym and scooted my feet into first position, already regretting my decision.

Sarah gave me a quick little nod and started the music. I went into my first move.

The sissonne.

Sarah didn't yell, so I turned, flowing into the double step.

I waited for her to scream something about my toes, but it never came.

So I pushed off with my foot and spun.

Not once.

Twice.

I planted my feet, catching myself before I fell. Sarah paused the song and stared at me. My entire body clenched, ready for the verbal bashing to start.

A tiny bit of me was hoping she'd really let loose. That way I could just look her in the eye and tell her *I quit.* Sabotage the whole competition right then and there. That way I could just go back to Kassie and apologize for ruining her plan and keep on being the dancer in the crew who couldn't actually dance.

Sarah's mouth went into a hard line like she was thinking.

"Well," she said.

Here it comes, I thought. *Be ready for it.*

"That was actually good."

My face went totally slack. "What?"

"It wasn't perfect, but it was a lot better."

I couldn't believe it. A compliment. About my dancing. From *Sarah.*

All the junk she had said before was still ringing in my ears. But it was getting quieter and quieter every second. Slowly being replaced by those two words.

Actually good.

I unclenched my fists, looking down at the little indentations my fingernails had made.

"Ready to learn the next part?" she asked.

More screaming. More trying to figure out her angle. More torture.

But also . . .

More moves. More technique. More real dancing.

I couldn't help it. I smiled.

And decided maybe I'd stick around a little while longer.

We finished practice with me learning the rest of my routine in small chunks.

Sarah recorded herself running it and messaged it to me later on. As soon as I got home, I ran to my room and played it. I had a mountain of reading homework I needed to get finished, but I couldn't stop watching her dance.

Thinking for a second that she was teaching me stupid moves was beyond idiotic.

The moves were incredible.

And the more I did them, the more incredible *I* felt.

It was starting to make having to say goodbye to it all in a raging inferno of *Ha! Take THAT, Dance-Splosion!* if I made into the top three even worse.

Over the next couple of days, I spent every second of free time at home practicing my routine. By Thursday I knew it by heart. Our football game that evening was an away game, so Sarah couldn't come. Hallelujah. She probably would've been yelling at me from the bleachers to quit slouching, shoulders down, long neck. Unfortunately, my friends weren't there, either. The only familiar faces in the stands were Mom and Dad.

So I kept my butt permanently attached to the bench. I wasn't really even paying attention to the game. All I could think about was the routine and how awesome it was.

The music would blast through the speakers during breaks and I ran through the steps in my head. The cheerleaders would kick and point toward the field and I pretended they were warming up for some sassy dance-off. The football players lined up for a play and I imagined they were posed, ready to bust out a choreographed routine.

But then DeMarcus would yell, "Hike!" and they'd all just fall over each other like they usually did. Which reminded me of all the times I'd nearly broken something on me or someone else during crew dance practice.

I glanced up at the scoreboard. We were losing pretty bad. Coach Bear had warned us about Oakdale. And

DeMarcus hadn't been kidding when he said the defensive end was a giant.

"No way that guy's in eighth grade." DeMarcus fell onto the bench beside me. "He's like three inches taller than last year."

"He's got a beard, too," I said, then remembered that the last time we spoke, I was sure I was going to walk away with a smashed nose. DeMarcus leaned forward, shaking the sweat off his face, and I moved down the bench as slowly as I could.

He looked over at me, eyebrows pinched together. "I smell bad or something?"

I froze mid-scoot. "No. You smell fine."

DeMarcus let out a weak-sounding laugh and sat up. "You still freaked out about the other day?"

"Yeah. I guess. Like maybe I feel bad for making you think I was calling you—"

"Whoa, easy." He swept his eyes around the sidelines really fast. "You can't just go throwing that word around, you know?"

"Um, not really."

"Guys don't like to hear it. Especially guys who have to change in the locker room with other guys. Even if— even if it's not true. You know?"

I sort of understood what he was saying. But at the same time totally didn't. "I was trying to say I know you're not. I mean, you're dating Sarah." I added that in more for me. Because I had enough to deal with. The thought of DeMarcus sending lovey-dovey texts to Kassie would just make me feel worse.

He sighed, staring out onto the field. "I don't know, man. It's . . . tough."

"Trust me, I know."

DeMarcus swiveled his head toward me. "You *do?*"

"Yeah. But I'm starting to get there. Or at least I think I am."

"So . . ." DeMarcus slid closer, his voice slipping into whisper mode. "How do you deal with it? Like, do you ever talk to your parents or anything?"

"Not really. I just sort of tell myself that I'll either get better or she'll lose her voice." I smiled at the thought of Sarah trying to bark out commands, but only managing a bunch of wimpy wheezes.

"Hold up." DeMarcus shook his head. "What're you talking about?"

"Sarah. How tough she is. I've been screamed at more these past few weeks than ever in my life."

His head fell forward. I thought he was going to pop back up and say something like *I feel you, man,* but instead he just sat there with his eyes closed and sighed. Maybe he liked my idea of Sarah not being able to talk and was praying that could happen for him, too.

"Are you okay?" I said.

He lifted his head. "I'm fine."

He wasn't. That much was obvious. What I couldn't get was why. "Hey, if you need to talk about something—"

"I said I'm fine," he snapped, and stood up, shaking out his hands. "I gotta get ready to go back in." He grabbed his helmet and walked toward the other first-string players, who were milling around on the sidelines.

I sort of wanted to go stand by him. Maybe try to get him to talk. If anything, maybe he could give *me* some pointers on how to survive Sarah. But I stayed put and tried to focus on the rest of the game.

Which we lost. By over thirty points. That was the bad news.

The good news was that practice was at my house on Saturday, so I got to sleep in later than usual. After we ran through our routine a few times, we sat down to get real-life zombified by Austin. He'd brought a makeup kit that he'd found online.

Carson sat on the edge of the end table, already halfway to undead as the YouTube video played back. He commented a few times, saying how much he liked some of the moves Sarah had taught me.

Kassie, though? Not so much.

"I'm not saying they don't look good," she said, shrugging. "Your lines really are looking better, but they're just not your style."

"They *could* be! I could just mix them in with my

old stuff. I could be like a contemporary ninja or something."

"Ooh, you could call it Kungtemporary Fu!" Carson said.

Austin snorted out a laugh, accidentally drawing a streak of green across Carson's forehead.

"Yes!" I said. "Kassie, think about it. It still works."

"But all you're doing is copying her moves. That's not what dance is about."

I plopped down on the couch beside her. I wanted to make sure she knew exactly how unfair I thought she was being.

She must have gotten the message. She sighed and leaned close so our arms were touching. "I just want you to be yourself. Because *that's* who I think is so awesome."

The frustration balled up on my face faded away and a smile broke through.

"So how bad is it?" Carson asked. "Working with the Wicked Witch of Sunnydale?"

"Like ninety percent of the time? Beyond awful." I didn't say how much I was actually loving all the stuff she was teaching me, though.

"Yeah, but she'll find a way to get you into the top three." Kassie pulled her feet up on the couch. "She's sneaky like that. Still not sure how she figured out I never sent in a video, though."

"Because she's a demon and has evil mind-reading powers," Carson said.

"Dude, stop moving before I poke you in the eye with this thing." Austin waved the little purple makeup stick in front of Carson.

"Well, she must not totally believe you didn't, because she's still helping me," I said.

Kassie nodded. Carson drew in a slow breath. "Ooh, if Sarah can read minds, I wonder what dirty thoughts she's picking up from Austin right now." Carson laughed, raising his hands like he was ready to block whatever Austin was going to throw at him. Kassie started making kissy sounds and I had to force myself not to stare at her lips while she did it.

"Okay, new rule." Austin set the tube of fake blood down. "No talking about Sarah or the plan or anything like that during the makeup test."

Carson rolled his eyes. "I'm really starting to worry about you, Austin. There are better girls at Sunnydale to crush on than Sarah Middleton."

"You know what? Maybe I don't care. Sarah's hot. She's got the bluest eyes I've ever seen and I think she smells good."

"She smells good?" Kassie asked, laughing behind her hand.

"Yes! She smells like ice cream. And I'm sort of tired

of hearing you all talk about how nasty she is. She's never been nasty to me."

"She's never been *anything* to you," Carson said. "I'm not sure she even knows you exist."

"She will one day. She'll look right at me. And she'll say hi."

Kassie shook her head, still smiling. "You're a freak, Austin. Which is why we love you. We won't talk about it when you're around, but I don't think we're changing our mind."

She looked at me like she was asking permission. I nodded. How could I stop after she'd admitted my lines were getting better? Sarah had said there'd be pain. I guess she meant it'd be going a lot deeper than just my muscles.

When I got to the gym on Monday for my next private lesson, Sarah was sitting on the bleachers, texting. The little clicks rattling from her phone sounded like a machine gun. "Change out of your dance gear."

"We not having practice?" A little tiny bubble of disappointment swelled in my chest. I'd actually been looking forward to showing her how much I'd practiced the routine.

"Not today."

"Why not?"

"Because I've been thinking about what you said about studios. And it's time you got un-brainwashed.

So call your parents. Tell them you might be late today."

Sarah stood up and shoved her phone in her back pocket.

"We're taking a field trip."

Me: ive been kidnapped by sarah HELP!

I was sitting in her dad's SUV and waiting for Kassie to text me back. When Sarah had told me where we were going, my stomach had turned to a lump of lead.

Dance-Splosion.

Where *real* dancers were made.

But it wasn't all the bad kind of nervousness. I'd always wanted to see the inside of a studio. Even more now that I was going to be sabotaging one of their contests. Thankfully, my parents needed some extra time to meet with some of their clients and had decided picking me up a little later wasn't a bad idea.

"So, Dillon, are you learning a lot working with Sarah?" Mr. Middleton asked.

Sarah stiffened up in the seat beside me like she was expecting me to make her look bad.

"Um, yeah. She's a pretty good teacher, I guess." I glanced at my phone again. No response. So I sent another message.

Me: she's taking me to dance-splosion what am i supposed to do?

"I'm better than pretty good, Dad," Sarah said. "Before he came to me, he didn't even know what a plié was, and now he's got an entire routine."

All he said back was, "Hm." Not like he was interested in what she'd said. More like someone had poked him in the gut and it just popped out of his mouth.

When I looked at Sarah, she was drawing something on a folder. *Arts eMotion* in big bubble letters. It reminded me of the Dizzee Freekz logo Kassie had made. "What's that?" I asked.

A big smile zipped across her face, then instantly disappeared when she glanced up toward the front seat. "Nothing."

"Is it like a crew name or something?"

She scooted over in her seat toward me. "It's the name of my studio." She was whispering, grinning while she did it. "Or it will be when I open it. After I graduate, of course."

"Cool. But you should put *Motion* in a different color."
Right as I said it, she shushed me.

Her dad's eyes flashed in the rearview mirror. "Sarah,"
he said calmly. But it was enough to send her sliding
toward the other side of the SUV in a huff. "We talked
about this. You're too good a dancer to work at a studio."

"That doesn't even make sense."

"It makes perfect sense. You're not going to waste
your skills—"

"It wouldn't be a waste, Dad!"

"Please don't interrupt me."

Sarah's mouth clamped shut. A miracle. But I couldn't
celebrate. Not when I was sitting in the middle of the
most uncomfortable situation ever.

"We've invested way too much time and money for
you to just throw everything away. In a couple of years
you'll be in a brand-new age group. You're going to have
to buckle down if you want a shot at nationals at that
level. So no more talk about teaching. That's not what
you've been trained for. Understand?"

Sarah nodded.

"Good." Mr. Middleton pushed a button on his Blue-
tooth headset and started up a conversation with someone on the other end.

Sarah's face was solid stone. Emotionless. Like she'd
sat in front of the mirror for hours practicing the *I'm
Sarah and there's nothing at all wrong* look. As she stared

out the window, I couldn't help but think how normal she looked when she was just sitting there not yelling at me. Almost like she was a totally different person than the Sarah I always saw walking with her Barbies and hanging off of DeMarcus. And then I wondered if she knew about what DeMarcus had asked me.

"What?" she asked, turning her head toward me like she was reading my mind.

"Oh, I— It's nothing."

"You were staring at me."

"No, I wasn't."

"I saw you in the window reflection."

Oops—busted. "I was just—" I checked to see if her dad was watching, but he was busy laughing with some invisible person. "I was just wondering how you and De-Marcus were doing."

Sarah's eyes flashed, surprised. It was quick, but I noticed. She looked back down at her phone. "We're fine. Why?"

"I don't know. I was just asking."

"Well, it's none of your business, so don't ask."

"It's my business if he talks to me."

She spun in her seat so fast I thought she was going to rip the seatbelt in half. "When did he talk to you? What'd he say?"

I shoved any thought of telling her the truth toward the back of my mind. The last thing I needed was a ticked-off quarterback *and* a ticked-off dance tutor. "Just football stuff. You know, games and plays and stuff. Nothing about you."

"You better not be spreading any rumors about him to your dork friends. You're not the only one who's got an image to protect, you know."

My head rocked backward like she'd just slapped me across the face. "I'm not! And his image is, like, perfect. He's the quarterback and he's dating *you*. He's basically the hero from every eighties movie."

Either she didn't hear me or didn't want to. She just went right back to her phone, scowling and texting a million miles an hour.

I didn't have to sit there for long, though. We pulled into the Dance-Splosion parking lot and my breath caught in my throat. The place was awesome. And way more intimidating in real life. DANCE was printed inside a big triangle that looked like a bloodred Dorito, and SPLOSION was in bright yellow letters on the brick.

A breathy "Whoa" escaped my lungs. Sarah shoved her phone back into her backpack and got out without saying a word. We were halfway to the building before I realized Mr. Middleton was still in the SUV. "Is your dad not coming in?" I asked.

She shook her head and pushed open the front door. "We won't be that long."

The inside was even fancier. The place had this warm

glow to it like everything had been carved out of gold. I passed by a poster that advertised the Heartland Dance Challenge. The same one where I was supposed to tear Dance-Splosion a new one. Just thinking about it sent a nervous tingle through my body.

"Hey, Sarah," the girl at the front desk said. She looked like she was probably in college. "You're here early."

"I'm just showing him around. This is Dillon. He sent in a video for the summer scholarship."

"Oh, hey, Dillon. I've heard a lot about you."

Sarah beamed me an *I told you so* smile.

"Well, good luck," the girl said. "If Sarah's rooting for you, then you must be pretty impressive."

Sarah waved and walked off. I followed her through a set of doors toward a hallway. "Okay, why are we really here?"

"Because you need to see what it's really like at a studio."

"Trust me, I've heard enough from Kassie."

Sarah stopped in her tracks. "That's the thing. She's put this idea in your head that studios are terrible, but they're not. It's just like at school when the teachers give you a ton of homework. They're doing it because it's supposed to help you get ready for high school."

Kassie had never put it that way. According to her, the bossiness was just a way for them to control the dancers. "So, um, do teachers really force all those moves on you?"

"That's called choreography, Dillon. It's a part of dance."

I nodded. So maybe Kassie *was* right.

"But they don't force it. They work with us. And sometimes we even get to suggest moves. The choreographer always has the final decision, but choreography's sort of this conversation between the dancer and the teacher. Like a partnership."

"What about all the rules? Doesn't that keep you from expressing yourself?"

Sarah rolled her eyes like she was already tired of my questions. "You can't dance without rules, Dillon. Dance is a sport. And sports have rules."

"But why? Dance is all about expression, and expression shouldn't need rules."

She pulled me down the hallway. "Take a look. The dancers here follow rules. They do what they're told and they dance what they're supposed to. You tell me. Are they not expressing themselves?"

I peeked in the windows as we passed, watching instructors model moves, dancers flowing in lines that were so straight it made a yardstick look curvy, and teams running routines in different styles. Contemporary, ballet, tap, hip-hop, jazz, everything.

It was incredible. I'd never seen so much dance in one place. And none of the students looked miserable. None of the teachers were snarling or foaming at the mouth like I halfway expected them to be.

It was just . . . dancing.

So. Much. Dancing.

The pictures from the website couldn't capture the epic level of technique I was seeing. If heaven was a dance studio, it would've looked like this.

Something was happening in my head. Like my brain was getting pulled in two.

On one side, Kassie's voice was telling me, *Don't listen to her, Dillon, she's lying! Studios are everything that's wrong with dance!*

On the other side, I heard Sarah. Telling me the exact opposite of everything I'd heard Kassie say.

When I'd fallen into this whole mess, I'd known exactly what I wanted. To get some dance help and sneak back out before things got complicated.

But now?

Seeing the big *what if?* staring back at me? Seeing real dancers in a real studio churning out moves that I only dreamed of doing?

I wasn't so sure anymore. The last thing I wanted to happen was to disappoint Kassie in some way. She was one of my best friends. And sometimes I wondered if we could be even more than that. But for the first time, I started to wonder if she wasn't telling me the whole truth about dance studios.

My head throbbed.

"Can we go? My parents are probably waiting on me."

"But I want to introduce you to the judges."

"No!" I blurted out. The last thing I needed was more reason to start doubting the direction I was supposed to be heading in. "They'll, um, be mad if I'm too late."

I could feel Sarah waiting for me to say why I really wanted to leave. But I couldn't. Finally she sighed, saying, "Fine. But that just means we'll have to work that much harder in practice."

We walked back to her dad's SUV. We didn't speak the entire way back to school. Not like we had anything to say. When we pulled back into the school parking lot, I got a reply from Kassie.

Kassie: OMG rly? have fun and don't come back a studio rat ROFL!

Reading it made me sick to my stomach.

Not because the idea of completely ditching Kassie's plan and actually trying to win disgusted me.

But because for the first time it didn't.

After Monday ended, my entire week was just a blur of school, football, and dance.

But there was one thing that kept breaking through the haze. One thing that wouldn't stop peeking out, whispering for me to come closer.

The scholarship.

At the end of summer, it'd been nothing more than a stupid idea.

But now it was a thought I couldn't shove away. Part of me regretted letting Sarah take me to Dance-Splosion. The other part couldn't stop thinking about it.

And all the dancing.

On Friday, my friends and our parents met at Davie's Diner to get mentally prepared for the dance-off. Mom and Dad sat with all the other parents. That was the good news.

The bad news?

"We finished it!" Kassie said, sliding a piece of paper in front of me as I sat down.

The speech.

Carson grabbed her arm excitedly. "We've been working on that all week. Austin was no help, by the way."

He shrugged. I would've been surprised if Austin *had* helped. The speech wasn't long, but they definitely didn't waste any words with their trash talking. There was stuff in there about how studios kill creativity, how the teachers only care about making money, even a line comparing the students to livestock. It was sort of horrible.

The parent table erupted into laughs at the back of the diner. We turned to see what was going on. My mom was standing up, wearing a homemade T-shirt that I guessed Carson's parents had made.

we love carson "c-note" evans!

All in puffy glitter-glue letters.

Carson's head fell into his arms. "Ugh, can I ride with one of you tomorrow?"

"Stop, they're just proud of you," Kassie said, giving my mom a thumbs-up.

"No, they're ruining my life. Do you know how embarrassing they are?"

"Geez, would you give it a rest?" I said. "They practically worship you, man. Seriously, I wish for once my big problem was that my mom and dad supported me a lot."

Carson's face went pale. Which was impressive, since he was already the color of milk. He pulled his arms into his lap and stared at the table.

A ball of regret instantly sprouted in my gut. "I'm sorry. It's none of my business." I sighed and slumped forward, almost stabbing myself in the eye on the ketchup bottle. "Please don't hate me."

"Nah," he said. "I can't stay mad at that face." He smiled. Not the usual full-mouth Carson smile, but at least it was something.

"Um—okay." Kassie cleared her throat. "Now that *that's* over. The speech. What do you think?"

I picked it up. "You really want me to say this? Onstage?"

"I mean, it doesn't have to be exactly that," Kassie said. "You can put your own words in. I'm sure you've got plenty to say after seeing the studio."

"Actually—" As soon as I said it, Kassie's smile disappeared. But I had to finish. If I didn't, I'd regret it. "It wasn't like that when I went. It was sort of okay. I mean, it wasn't, like, perfect or anything, but—"

"Oh, well, I'm glad you didn't think the dance studio

was perfect." Kassie shoved her back against the booth. "It's just the one place that almost made me want to quit dancing, is all."

"Whatcha guys wanna drank?" the waitress asked, sneaking up on us.

We each told her, and when she asked if we were ready to order our food, Carson said, "You should probably give us a minute. Or five." As soon as the waitress left, he leaned forward. "Are you forgetting something? Sarah knows Kassie's not competing. Which means she's just stringing you along for whatever reason."

"I don't think she is, though," I said, peeling off a layer of the napkin in my hand.

"Then why would she keep helping you?"

I shrugged. "Maybe she actually wants me to win."

"Yeah, right," Carson said.

"Look, I'm not saying what Dance-Splosion did to Kassie was right, because it wasn't. Like, at all. I'm just saying maybe the place has changed. Maybe we don't really need to sabotage the contest."

"I'm with Dill," Austin said. "I never thought we needed to anyway."

Kassie beamed him a narrow-eyed glare. "Yeah. We know, Austin."

"Can we not do this right now?" Austin shoved his glasses up his nose. "Tomorrow's the dance-off. We need to stay focused and positive and junk."

"I'm not the one who's in love with Dance-Splosion all of a sudden."

"Kassie, I'm not . . ." I dragged my hands down my face.

I *wasn't* in love with Dance-Splosion. But after seeing what the place was really like, I just wasn't mortal enemies with it anymore. Plus, Austin had a point. The last thing we needed was to go into tomorrow's contest all weird and mad at each other. I scooted in the booth closer to Kassie.

"Look. You're right," I said, looking down at the speech. "I only saw a piece of the studio. You're the one who spent all that time in there."

Kassie slowly relaxed. Austin's mouth fell open, probably ready to ask why I'd just changed my mind. I kicked him under the table before he could.

"So you're not going to dump us for a studio, then?" A tiny smile worked its way onto the corners of her mouth.

I held a hand out, palm down, above my head—"Dizzee Freekz"—and another one way below the table—"Dance-Splosion." Austin was still staring at me, looking completely betrayed, so I added, "And we'll have all summer long to work on Austin's movie."

"Good answer," Carson said.

Kassie nodded. "Exactly. Especially since I do *not* want to miss seeing Carson decked out in zombie makeup."

Carson ran an imaginary comb through his blond hair.

"I'll be the most fabulous undead you've ever seen. Like James Dean. No! James *Dead*."

"Who's James Dean?" Austin asked.

"Seriously? You want to be a director and you don't know?"

Austin looked at me. I shrugged. I had no idea who the guy was, either.

When the waitress came back, we each put in an order. Kassie warned us to go light on the meal, but I didn't listen. I had about a million things I was worrying about and I needed to bury them all under a chili cheeseburger with onion rings.

Fortunately, it worked.

Unfortunately, the lump of food stayed wadded up in my stomach all the way until morning.

When we got to the mall the next day, I almost asked Mom and Dad to carry me inside. Even the swishing motion of walking made the inside of my stomach boil.

The food court had a small stage set up right in the middle of it. I got a whiff of something cooking over at the Frank-N-Furters stall. Not good. I ran over to a garbage can, ready to say goodbye to the corn nuggets I'd ordered halfway through dinner. But I forced my stomach to go back into hibernation mode.

"Dillon! Over here!" Kassie yelled.

She was standing in a wide hallway at the back of the food court. There was a tall piece of cloth strung up behind her, with a pair of dressing room signs over two curtain doors. One for boys and one for girls.

"Dude, look at what her mom made!" Austin handed me a pin. It was about as wide as a soda can top and had Kassie's Dizzee Freekz design printed on it.

"That is so cool!" I said.

"Thanks," Kassie said. "I sort of stole Austin's business card idea."

"I'm just glad you put the YouTube link on them." Austin reached into Kassie's backpack and pulled out a handful of pins. "I'm gonna go pick out a good spot to film and pass these out to people." He yanked his half mask down and disappeared into the crowd of mall-walking senior citizens and kids on leashes.

"Thanks for doing that for him," I said.

"I want people to see our dances. We're a good crew." Kassie smiled and my heart instantly tore in two. But I guess that's what I deserved for giving Dance-Splosion permission to crawl inside my head. I'd imagined myself in some of those classes about a million times. And in each one, there wasn't a shred of ninja freestyling. Just real moves. Real technique.

Kassie pointed to the guys' side of the dressing room. "You better go get changed. Carson's already in there."

I walked in, expecting a room full of tall, deerlike dancers to be decked out in unitards and sequined shirts. But the only people in there were Carson and some old janitor with a broom.

"Where's everyone else?" I asked, pulling out my football pants and mask.

"This is it," Carson said. "Unless everyone's taking the fashionably late approach."

When we finished suiting up, we walked back out into the hallway. Kassie pulled the bottom of my shirt down. Her hand grazed my butt and I almost yelped like a Chihuahua.

"At least the stain's nearly gone," she said, nodding and walking off. Thankfully, my face was hidden behind a ninja mask. If it hadn't been, the entire mall would've seen it go supernova red.

The stage was about a foot off the ground, sort of like the one our school dragged out when we had assemblies. The entire backdrop was an ad for Smoothietopia and had a picture of a family all smiling and laughing, holding their not-even-touched smoothies.

The announcer walked to the middle and grabbed the microphone. He was an older guy dressed in a full suit with no tie. His shirt was unbuttoned enough so a poof of chest hair stuck out. He tapped his microphone and the crowd quieted down. "Ladies and gentlemen, welcome to the first annual Smoothietopia Dance-Off!"

I spotted the tiny table in front with the judges. A man and a woman, both wearing Smoothietopia polos.

"We have a great show for you today. And remember, the winners each get a twenty-dollar gift certificate to Smoothietopia, where the only thing sweeter than your first smoothie is your next one!" He laughed like their slogan was the cutest thing he'd ever heard. "And judging today's competition we have Mr. and Mrs. Smoothie-topia, Vincent Damico and Margaret Goldman!"

They stood and waved. I'd seen their pictures on the commercials. Good to know we were about to get judged by a pair of milkshake experts.

"So let's get started, everyone! Be sure to cheer on your favorites, and don't forget to stop by Smoothie-topia on the way home today!"

A bored-looking girl wearing a headset walked over to us. "You competing today?"

"Yeah," Kassie said. "We're the Dizzee Freekz. I already signed us up." I could hear the worry in her voice.

"Okay. Follow me." She led us behind the stage. "So what's with the masks? Your faces all burnt or something?" the girl said, smacking a piece of chewing gum.

"Uh, no. It's just part of our costumes. I'm the Kung Fu Kid." I pointed at the others while I fastened my new Dizzee Freekz pin to my shirt. "And that's Misstik and C-Note. Dr. Doom's in the audience filming—"

"Whatever," the girl said, rolling her eyes. "Stay back here. I'll give you the thumbs-up when it's your turn."

She walked off and parked herself at the corner of the stage. The butterflies in my stomach were shaking the morning puke from their wings and fluttering around. I took a deep breath and looked at the rest of my crew. Nobody spoke. They looked about as nervous as I felt.

"Okay, Sunnydale Mall, put your hands together and help me welcome our first contestants. The Geriatrics!"

Some soft, jazzy music started up and I poked my head around the corner to check out our competition. A bunch of old people. And one of them was the janitor I'd seen in the changing room. He still had his broom and was shuffling around behind four old ladies in dresses.

For a bunch of grandmas, they were pretty lively. They'd do a little turn here, a little kick there. Wiggle right, jiggle left, smile to the crowd, let Gramps pop out in front to dip the broom like a dancer. Not bad at all.

The crowd applauded and the silver-headed dancers took a bow. I turned back around. The others were right behind me, watching.

"They were so cute!" Carson said.

Kassie stepped back, shaking out her hands. "Okay, we're third on the list. One more and we'll be up."

We rushed back to the edge of the stage. About a dozen men and women walked up, each one carrying a tiny baby. The adults sat down in a line, placing the toddlers in front of them.

"And now, for our second act, please welcome the Eastbrook Community Center's 'My Baby and Me' Program!"

A bunch of people in the crowd jumped up, cheering like they were at a concert. A cutsey-pootsy song with way too many cartoon sound effects blared out over the speakers, and the babies waved back and forth, sidestepping and hopping. Of course, their parents were doing all the work. The most I saw one of the little ones do was try to stick an entire foot in his mouth and then ugly-cry when it wouldn't fit.

My eyes met Austin's and we both exchanged a *What in the world is going on?* expression. The song ended and the moms and dads walked offstage with the babies in tow. The girl with the headset gave us an unenthusiastic thumbs-up.

"Okay, guys," Kassie said, huddling us up. "This is it. Let's get out there and blow their minds."

Carson and I nodded, both giving Kassie a high five at the same time.

I took all the stray thoughts that had to do with the scholarship, the studio, and Kassie's plan and wadded them up in the back of my mind. I didn't have time to worry about that stuff.

The Kung Fu Kid had some faces to melt.

The announcer glanced at the stack of cards in his hands. "And for our last performance today—"

Me and Carson looked at each other like we were both asking the same question: *Did he say "last"?*

"—the . . . Dizzy . . . Freakies!" The announcer stumbled over the name like he was trying to read a foreign language.

I waited for Kassie to react, too, but she was in the zone. Eyes closed, breathing controlled, shoulders relaxed. Her skin looked almost golden under the food court lights. I took a deep breath, visualizing my toes pointing, my legs straight, and my shoulders lowered. I imagined a long neck and loose hands. Sarah had told me I danced with my hands too clenched up, but when I told her that's because I do all those punches, she'd remind me that I shouldn't be doing all those punches.

Too bad there wasn't a French dance word for *ninja attack*.

We all took our spots. My parents were in the third row and Mom had her phone out, recording everything.

I tested out my calves. Not too bad. It didn't look like Kassie was having any trouble, either. She was spinning in place like a ballerina in a music box, her black curls trying to keep up.

My eyes found her face. She never wore makeup. She didn't need any. She'd rock the dark eyeliner every now and then at school, but never when she danced. No, when she was moving to music, she was just Kassie. No glitter, no product. Just—

I shook my head.

What was I doing? I'd missed my cue! I jumped in, already half a beat behind. I cut out a jump to make up for lost time and hit my mark behind Kassie. I was supposed to grab her arms, but I hesitated. My hands were sweaty. She was wearing a sleeveless T-shirt and I didn't want to gross her out. Kassie leaned left and I snapped my hands up, forcing them down on her shoulders. She'd felt my sweaty hands a million times before. Why was I all of a sudden so worried about it?

Sarah's drill-sergeant scream clawed into my brain. *CONCENTRATE, STUPID! AND POINT YOUR TOES!*

I spun, forcing my back into a stiff-as-a-board position. Normally I'd land and whip out a series of jabs and chops. I raised my arms, ready to hack the air in front of me. And hesitated. Real dancers didn't punch.

Nothing I'd learned from Sarah would've fit, so I sliced through a field of imaginary boards toward the other end of the stage. Except I let my hands fall loose like Sarah had taught me. It felt so wrong. It looked like I was swatting away a wasp. My hands flapped and wiggled through the air like I had pieces of uncooked bacon on the ends of my wrists.

I caught a glimpse of Carson. He'd just come out of a spin and he was frowning, watching me wiggle around the stage like a moron. I pulled my arms back down. No more punches. I lowered my shoulders and wedgie-walked over to Kassie. I even added in a sissonne.

It didn't feel half bad.

Didn't feel half good, either.

Especially since I was so busy trying to be stiff and professional that I landed on Kassie's foot.

She growled, pulled her shoe free, and side-glided away. I mirrored her moves as best I could, but it was no use. My mind was as far away from the music and the rhythm as it could possibly be. For the next two and a half minutes, I stumbled through moves, second-guessing every step I made. The only thing I didn't mess up was when we all froze at the end.

The music faded out. Besides the applause from our parents, the most we got from the crowd was a few shrugs and the *I guess we should clap* sort of clapping. We left the stage. The announcer was blabbering on about Smoothietopia and a small break so the judges could make their decision. Not like we had anything to worry about. We were dead last because of me.

Kassie pulled me to the side. "Stop it," she said, glaring.

"What?"

"Stop stomping around like that. You did great out there."

I gave her the *Are you being serious right now?* look. She glanced at Carson like she was waiting for him to back her up.

"Oh, yeah," he finally said. "You did your best. I think. That's all that matters."

"Whatever. I don't have a *best*. I don't even have a *pretty good*." I leaned hard against the back of the stage, making the entire thing wobble.

Our first and only dance competition and I'd ruined it.

An achy pinch gripped my throat and I almost lost it. I turned my head away. They didn't care about winning, but still. Letting them down over and over hurt more than a calf cramp.

Flashes of the Dance-Splosion dancers filled my brain. My head was a ping-pong ball, getting smacked back and forth between a scholarship and a speech.

Kassie's voice broke through it all, making me jump. "I really am," she said.

"Huh? You're what?" I blinked a few times, trying to get the burned-in image of the floor tiles to melt away.

"Proud, you dork. I'm proud of us all. I mean, we put ourselves out there and we should be happy with that."

"I'm not," I said. "I messed up our routine. I messed up everything. We're gonna come in dead last and it's all my fault."

Carson slid the fox mask up on top of his head. "Dillon, you didn't mess up anything. You danced. You can't mess up dancing."

Austin came walking around the corner, watching the footage on his camera. "Do I have to use this footage? Because Dillon looks like he's having a seizure in most of it."

Kassie slapped his arm, shushing him.

"See?" I said. "I *can* mess up dancing. I broke every dance rule out there."

"Rules?" Kassie said. "Who told you dance has— Oh, never mind." Kassie held out her hand. I grabbed it and she yanked me to my feet. "Dance is an art, Dillon. There are no rules to art. And we don't care about winning. If we get a trophy, then cool. But it's not why we do this. We do this because we're proving to everyone out there it doesn't matter what junk some big studio tries to teach you. If you don't love it, then it doesn't mean anything."

I pried the wad of football pants out of my crack just as the microphone squealed out a quick burst of feedback.

"Well, ladies and gentlemen, we have our winner," the announcer said.

I sat back down. Knowing I was about to hear we lost to either a group of babies or a group of old people made me sick to my stomach. Kassie sat down beside me. Our knees were touching, but it only made me feel a little better.

"It was a close one, folks. Only two points between first and second place. But the winners of our first annual Smoothietopia Dance-Off are—"

I slid my fingers into my ears to block it out. And it worked. Except Kassie jumped up, scaring me so bad that I yanked my fingers out to hear her screaming.

My first thought was that she was crying.

But she wasn't. She was cheering.

She looked at me and I immediately knew . . .

We won!

I couldn't believe it. I wrapped a hug around Kassie without even thinking. As soon as I did, I pulled my arms back, halfway expecting her to draw her face up in disgust. But she didn't. She bit the corner of her bottom lip. Smiled. Pushed that one stray curl behind her ear. Amazing.

"This is crazy! Come on, guys!" Carson said, pulling us toward the stage.

"There they are, folks," the announcer said as we walked up, putting our masks back on. "Our winners!" He let the already dwindling clapping come to a complete stop. "Let's introduce you three to the audience. How about you all take the masks off so we can see—"

"No thanks!" I blurted out, getting a few giggles from the crowd.

"Well, that's no problem. So, your names?" He stuck the mike under Kassie's face.

"I'm Misstik."

"You can call me C-Note!"

I cleared my throat. "The Kung Fu Kid."

The announcer let out a fake-sounding laugh. "Well, okay. Now, on behalf of our sponsor, we'd like to present your team with these Smoothietopia gift certificates, good for one year at any participating Smoothietopia."

The girl with the headset shoved a piece of paper in each of our hands and walked offstage.

"So," the announcer said, turning toward us. "Are you ready to take your show on the road?"

"Um, yeah. I guess," Kassie said. "As long as we get to dance."

"Well, don't worry, young lady. You will. Because as a special prize, we're sending each of you to your next competition. And it's one we're very proud to be a sponsor of for the very first time. Hosted by Davis County High School, home of the Blue Devils, your next stop on the dance train is—" He smiled, leaving us frozen as we hung on the edge, waiting for him to say the next words.

And then he did.

"The Heartland Dance Challenge in November!"

We all turned toward Kassie.

But she was already running off the stage.

▲▲▲▲▲▲▲▲▲

We finally found Kassie hiding in the dressing room.

"Kass, what's going on?" Carson said, poking the curtain door.

Austin cupped his mouth and shouted, "Yeah, was your mask on too tight? We won!"

I pulled his hand down. "It's a curtain. You don't have to yell."

Carson spun around to face us. "What if she's having girl issues? Maybe we should give her some space."

"I'm pretty sure it has to do with what that announcer said, Carson."

Austin cupped his mouth again. "Is it girl issues?"

Before I could say anything, Kassie ripped the door open, making us all jump. Her mask was off. The level of freak-out on her face was almost scary.

"What's wrong?" I asked. She was staring at something behind me. I looked and saw her parents standing there. I jogged over to them.

"Is she all right?" her dad asked in his thick French accent. "She just ran off."

"Yeah, she's okay. We're just, uh, having a crew meeting is all." I didn't wait for them to answer. I went back to the dressing room. Carson and Austin were already inside. I stepped inside and almost froze to death. The look Kassie was giving everyone was beyond frigid. She was standing at the back of the little room with her arms crossed.

"I still don't get it. This is what you've been waiting for," Carson said.

Kassie just shook her head. "Sorry. I've already made up my mind."

"Made up your mind to do what?" I asked.

"The next contest. She said she 'can't' do it," Austin said, putting a pair of air quotes around the word *can't*.

This was bad. As soon as the announcer had mentioned the competition, the plan had formed in my head. A way to come out of this mess in one piece. "Why can't you?"

"I just can't, okay? You're going to have to trust me, guys." Kassie turned her head away.

"See?" Austin said, and sat down beside Carson.

"But this is too perfect!" I said. "Think about it,

Kassie. Instead of me getting up onstage by myself and completely ruining Sarah's life, we can all dance together."

Austin jumped up. "Dude, yes! Kassie, you guys have to do this. It's a way better plan, no offense."

"Are you all just not listening?" Kassie's arms fell to her sides. "I can't get up on that stage and dance. Not this time. And I'm not trying to ruin Sarah's life, Dillon." The way my name flew out of her mouth made me take a step back.

"Wait a minute," Carson said. "Are you saying you *can't* dance, or are you saying you just don't *want* to?"

"Does it matter?"

"Yes, it matters. Kassie Gilbert doesn't *want* to dance all of a sudden? I don't believe that for a second."

"Does this have to do with what Sarah did to you?" I asked.

Kassie's head whipped around to me. Bingo.

"What're you not telling us? Because Carson's right, you not wanting to get up onstage and dance just sounds backward."

"I'm not hiding anything."

"Yes, you are, Kassie."

Her eyes were red. Kassie might not want to hurt Sarah, but what she and Carson had planned for me definitely would.

"If you don't want to go through with it, then fine,"

she said. Carson's mouth fell open like he was ready to object. "I'm serious. Just quit taking private lessons with Sarah and we'll forget the whole thing. No plan. No speech. No hurting anyone."

I caught a glimpse of Austin nodding furiously beside me. Kassie's solution was perfect. It solved pretty much every problem I could think of.

Or *almost* every problem.

"Couldn't we maybe forget the plan without me quitting the lessons?"

"I knew it!" Kassie yelled, jabbing a finger at me. "You *want* to get into Dance-Splosion!"

"No, I—it's not like that, I swear!"

She leaned her head back on the wall, staring at the ceiling. "Then can I ask you one question?"

I nodded, then realized she couldn't see me since she was still looking up. "Yeah."

"Do you actually want to go for that scholarship?" Kassie's eyes floated down to me.

My heart rocked against my chest so hard I almost stumbled. I tried to take in a breath, but I couldn't. It was like my body was turning against me. Carson and Austin were staring, waiting for an answer. I wanted to be honest with them. I just didn't know what the honest answer actually *was*.

"It's complicated," I said.

The skin on the front of Kassie's neck darkened. "That's another way to say yes."

"No, it's not."

"You said the crew came first. Were you just lying?"

"I wasn't lying, Kassie."

"You said you didn't want the scholarship, but you actually do. How is that *not lying*, Dillon?"

"Because I don't know if I want it! All you and Carson have ever told me is how awful studios are. That dance is just expression. And now Sarah's telling me all about rules and technique and stuff. What if a studio can help me? What if they could make me a real dancer?"

"You *are* a real dancer," Carson said.

"No, I'm not. And every time I try to get you all to teach me some real moves, you won't. I'm sick of looking like an idiot dancing with you guys."

"Dude, you just won first place in a dance contest," Austin said. "I kinda think that means your dancing's good enough."

"How would you know, Austin? You're not even a dancer! All you do is turn the camera on and off!" My mouth mashed shut right after I'd said it. But it was too late. Ever since Austin started recording our practices, I'd tried extra hard to make him feel like he belonged. And I'd just ruined it in less than five seconds. "I didn't mean—"

"Whatever, dude." Austin grabbed his camera. "I'm out." He stormed past the curtain door, ignoring Carson and Kassie begging him to stay.

When I turned back around, they were glaring at me like I was a stranger.

"I didn't mean to yell. I just—need some time to think. I think."

Kassie looked at me with a pair of red, teary eyes. It was like my heart opened up at the top and someone dumped in a bucket of hot coals. If I was having a heart attack, I didn't care. All I could think about was how I'd hurt my team. How I'd hurt *her*.

"I love the Dizzee Freekz. I swear. I want you to know that." I took a step toward the exit. Slowly, waiting for her to say something.

All I got was a curtained room full of silence.

I grabbed the strip of fabric that pretended to be a door and realized I'd left my certificate on the bench behind me. Before I could decide whether or not to just leave it there, someone slid it into my hand.

"You forgot this," Kassie said.

I turned. Her pinky was touching mine. I didn't want to pull the certificate free and lose the tingly feeling racing up my arms. I would've stood there, eyes locked on our hands, forever. But I noticed she already had her bag slung over her shoulder.

"Later," she said, and walked out. Carson went by and I could practically feel the angry steam about to start shooting out his ears.

I waited a while before I left. I couldn't stand the

thought of walking behind them, wondering if they were going to go home and FaceTime each other, talking about how disappointed they were in me.

Then I realized I was standing in what was technically a girls' dressing room and decided I should probably be all paranoid somewhere else.

▲ ▲ ▲

The only good thing about that next Monday was the fact they had chicken tenders at lunch. Those were my favorite. But after the first bite, I stopped eating. My stomach was too busy balling itself into a tiny lump. Especially after almost running into Kassie in the lunch line.

Thankfully, she didn't see me.

Not that it made me feel any better.

But at least I wasn't the only one who looked miserable. DeMarcus had his head propped up on one hand and was swirling a piece of chicken around in a puddle of honey mustard sauce with the other. The other players never noticed.

I cleared my throat, trying to get his attention, but he never looked up. I tried again and earned a fifty-pound elbow from Troy.

"If you're sick, go sit somewhere else, Tighty Whitey. I don't wanna catch your germs."

I decided to take his advice. I wasn't sick, but the

last place I wanted to be was wedged between him and Bobby Fleagle. As soon as I stood up, Sarah and her Barbies dropped their trays on the table. Her face was stuck in an openmouthed smile. "You better be thanking me right now, Dillon."

"Uh, you may want to sit down. We don't want you fainting all over the table," Red-Haired Barbie said.

So I did. "What am I thanking you for exactly?"

Sarah held her phone out to me. A text message.

Becky: hey grl im not sposed to say nething yet but i heard ur boi made the cut!!!

My heart sped up so much it threatened to rip through the front of my shirt. I read the text a few more times, making sure I wasn't missing something in all the abbreviations.

"What is it?" DeMarcus said, finally lifting his head.

All I could do was shake my head, not even able to believe what I was reading.

"Don't get weird. You didn't win," Sarah said, and showed DeMarcus the message. "Some girl at the studio heard Dillon made it to the top three."

"Congrats, man," DeMarcus mumbled.

I told him thanks, but my body was refusing to be happy about it. The idea of winning was awesome. Only when it stayed an idea, though. Because an idea was harmless. An idea wasn't going to tear me away from my best friends.

But the idea had just become a real possibility.

I sat there gripping the edge of the table so hard my knuckles ached. "This wasn't supposed to happen."

"Excuse me?" Sarah said.

"I said, um—" I tried to swallow, but my mouth had turned into a desert. "I can't believe this is happening." My eyes darted over to DeMarcus. He was staring at me like he knew what I'd really said.

Apparently Sarah didn't, though. "Well, it is. And you're welcome. Now, the finalist auditions are in three weeks, so we need to get your routine as flawless as—" She snapped her fingers in front of my face, making me flinch. "Dillon, pay attention."

"Yeah, what's your problem?" Black-Haired Barbie said. "Why are you acting all pouty?"

"I'm not. I just don't want to hurt anyone is all."

"How would you hurt someone? You're going to be dancing in front of the judges, not doing brain surgery on them."

"I just don't want to make my friends hate me."

Troy reached over and messed up my hair with his hand. "Aww, I didn't know Tighty Whitey was such a sensitive little guy!"

I tried to squirm away, but Bobby kept pushing me back over to him, laughing.

"Will you two stop?" Sarah hissed. "Every time you lift your arms I feel like I want to puke."

Troy and Bobby sniffed their armpits and looked at each other, shrugging.

"We've already talked about this, Dillon. You have to do what it takes to win. And if they never talk to you again—" She shook her head and pushed her tray away. "Then maybe they were never your friends to begin with."

Weird hearing that coming from the girl who'd practically admitted to stepping all over her friends. But even weirder was how much sense it made.

Sarah shrugged. "Like I already said. Dance is a sport. You can't win without making some people mad."

Somehow I made it through the rest of the day alive. Practice with Sarah was the quietest it had ever been. We ran the routine over and over. I stepped, I extended, I leaped, I reached. I did all the moves I was supposed to.

My feet were pointier than ever. My legs straighter. I never fell out of a single spin. The dance winds were blowing me toward the scholarship faster than I ever thought they would. And all I could think about was how bad I felt. Every step I took toward Dance-Splosion was one step away from the Dizzee Freekz.

But if I jumped overboard now and tried to swim back?

I could be kissing my chance of ever becoming a real dancer goodbye.

During the week, I texted Austin like a hundred times and never got more than a one- or two-word answer back from him.

Me: u ok man? i didn't mean to hurt ur feelings.
Austin: im fine.
Me: i rly think ur videos are awesome.
Austin: thnx.

And I didn't want to text Kassie or Carson, either. Not yet. I think I was scared I'd get less than a couple of words. Or maybe I'd get a lot more and they'd be something I wouldn't want to read.

The game on Thursday didn't pull me out of my funk. Kassie, Carson, and Austin were all there. Normally that'd make me sitting on the bench feel almost tolerable.

But not now.

I turned around and accidentally caught Kassie's eyes. She had herself buried in her hoodie. She gave me the smallest wave a human arm could give. I waved back and turned around to pretend to watch our team continue to thrash Dogwood Middle.

On Friday, she sent a text to everyone reminding us that we didn't have practice on Saturday. Her great-grandmother was turning ninety-three and her family was driving up to Kentucky to visit her in the nursing home.

I should've been bummed I wouldn't be dancing with my friends. Honestly, though? I wasn't sure if I would've been able to show up.

Yeah, I missed them. But the Kung Fu Kid was stuck in the middle of a fight between the Dizzee Freekz and Dance-Splosion.

And he was tired of getting his butt kicked.

16

The worst part about having parents who entertained their business clients at home was that I always got stuck cleaning.

Sure, my mom and dad helped, but it still wasn't fair. Especially since this time they were making me clean out a closet. In the basement.

"Are we planning on giving them a tour or something?" I asked Dad as I pulled out a box of some of my old junk.

"No. But we may play some hide-and-seek, so we need this cleaned out."

"Can you imagine Mom trying to stay quiet enough for that?" I asked. "After like ten seconds, she'd be yelling at someone to come find her."

Dad laughed. "I'm telling her you said that."

"So who's coming over?" I asked as I dug through my stuff. "It's not that old lady who does the knitting, is it? She smells like cat food."

"No, it's Alan."

"The penny guy?"

"He's not just buying—" Dad groaned, tossing a stack of cracked plastic bowls onto the trash pile. "Yes. Alan. The *old coin* guy."

"Mom's idea?"

He nodded. "But we need his business. I know his idea sounds weird, but it can make us a lot of money. Don't worry, though. I've already told him to prepare for the Spanish Inquisition." He said the last two words in a high-pitched British voice.

"The what?"

"The— Never mind. Just be ready for a very long dinner."

By the time Alan finally showed up, my stomach was about ready to chew its way through my shirt. Mom cooked chicken Parmesan and the smell filled every inch of the house. Alan didn't look like a guy who'd think buying up pennies was a good idea. He looked more like an elementary school principal. Short, skinny, with a smile that stretched almost as wide as his bow tie.

While I ate, I kept eyeballing Mom, waiting for her

to say something about pennies. But she never did. The conversation sort of rolled around, touching on the food before bouncing to the weather and then all the construction on Interstate 40.

Eventually, it landed on sports.

"So, Dillon," Alan said, wiping his mouth. "Your dad says you play football?"

I nodded.

"What position?"

Was *bench* a position? Before I could come up with something, Dad butted in. "He's got his eye on a few different ones right now." He winked at me.

"This might be my last year, actually," I said, staring at the pile of green beans in front of me. Someone's fork scraped across their plate. I looked up. "I want to concentrate more on my dancing."

Alan's eyebrows slowly inched up his forehead. "Dancing?" He glanced at Dad like he was waiting for him to translate. "Never mentioned dancing."

"Dillon's on a dance crew," Mom said, smiling. "He's up for a scholarship to Dance-Splosion."

"So, you . . ." Alan set his napkin down. "You're a ballet dancer?"

"No," I said. "I don't have, like, anywhere near the skills for that. I'm learning contemporary. I also do some hip-hop. Sort of."

The old guy's face pinched up like he was confused.

Dad started to say something, but Mom cut him off. "Lots of boys dance, Alan."

He laughed. "Oh, sure they do. I'm just a little surprised you're letting Dillon do it, though."

"Why?" I asked, only halfway trying to keep my voice at a normal, calm level.

"Uh, I think what Alan's trying to say is, um—" Dad cleared his throat and put on a smile. "It's just a little unusual. For boys to dance, I mean."

"No, it's not."

"No, not unusual," Alan said. "Maybe a little risky, though."

He had a point. Dancing with me wasn't always the safest best. But I was getting better. I hadn't fallen into a bookshelf in weeks. "Football's risky, too. In our last game, some guy broke his finger so bad it was bent all backwards."

"Dillon, not while we're eating, honey," Mom said.

Alan propped his elbows on the table. "I'm talking about different kinds of risk. I was the assistant principal at a middle school for eleven years." Nailed it. Almost. "Trust me, kids can be pretty ruthless. Chuck, you get what I'm saying, right? About it being risky?"

Mom shot to her feet. "Okay, how about coffee? Coffee, anyone?"

Later on, after Alan left, Dad came up to my room, where I was trying to do my homework. But all I could think about was Alan and his comments.

"Maybe Alan's right," Dad said, sitting on my bed. "You'll be in high school before you know it. I can't imagine boy dancers have it very easy at that age."

I put down my pencil. "Nobody cares if boys dance, Dad. When Sarah took me to Dance-Splosion, there were tons of guys there."

He held up his hands, trying to calm me down. "Okay, but still. Boys who dance get called a lot of things, Dillon. I don't want you to have to go through that."

"I don't go through that, though. And even if they did call me names, I wouldn't even care."

"But *I* would. And so would your mom."

It finally made sense. He wasn't scared of what it'd do to me if I got called names for dancing. He was scared of how embarrassed he'd be for having the son who pranced around onstage instead of sitting on the sidelines during the football games.

"I just want you to be safe," he said. "And I guess dancing does seem like sort of a risky hobby to have."

My face tensed up so hard I was surprised my forehead didn't rip. "Good to know you care."

During the week, I made myself forget about the whole Alan-the-penny-buying-jerk incident. I used every second of my spare time to run routines after school. I was hoping I'd have one of those lightbulb moments where it all suddenly seemed so clear. And I was *really* hoping it'd come before practice on Saturday. But instead, thinking about what my dad said just made things worse and put me into a seriously bad mood. I kicked my dresser, sending my toe into a concussion.

I hopped around the room trying to muffle the bad words coming out of my mouth. Apparently it didn't work, because around the sixth or seventh one, someone knocked on my door.

"Dillon, are you okay?"

I sat down on my bed, staring at the damage. It felt way worse than it looked. "Yeah. Just trying to find the piece of my foot I just broke off."

The door opened and Mom came in. She put her palm on my face. Like she could tell how bad the injury was by feeling whether or not I had a fever.

"What happened?"

"Nothing. Just banged my toe a little." Or a lot.

"Okay. If you're sure." Mom smoothed my hair away from my eyes.

I shoved my backpack out of the way and spotted the Dizzee Freekz pin I'd attached to one of the straps. "Mom, can I ask you something?"

"Sure, sweetie."

"Okay." I took a deep breath. "Let's say there's this— gum you like. I mean you *love* it. Can't go a day without chewing it. But the more you chew it with your friends, the more the flavor gets sort of lost. And then someone offers you a different flavor."

Her eyes grew wide.

"So you try it and it's good, too. *Really* good. But you

know if you start chewing that kind, it'll make your friends hate you. Which one do you choose?"

Mom sat on the edge of my bed and grabbed my hand. "Sweetie, is this about drugs?"

"What? No! Mom, it's about—gum. Just gum."

She let out a long sigh of relief. "Good. That's good. But you understand if someone offered you drugs—"

"Mom, seriously. No one's offering me drugs. I swear."

She narrowed her eyes. "Okay. Because your father and I—"

I fell back on my bed with the loudest moan I could manage. This was pointless. Why were parents so stubborn? "All I want to know is what gum to choose, Mom!"

"Okay, okay. I'm sorry." She held her hands up like she was offended. "If this is just about gum, and I had to choose? I'd always choose the one that made me the happiest."

"What about if you know it'll hurt someone?"

"Then you talk to that person. And if they're a real friend, they'll understand." She stood, picked up my laundry basket, and opened my door. "If all through school I'd just done what others wanted me to do, I'd have never married your father."

That evening I finally got the official email saying I was a finalist and what to expect for the second round of auditions and how proud I should be of myself for making it this far.

Proud.

I should've been.

Not sure how I was supposed to reach past the guilt to pull that emotion free, though.

▲ ▲ ▲

By Friday morning, the pain was nearly gone. Both pains. The watermelon-sized knot my toe had turned into was going to take a little while longer to heal, but the volcano-hot fist that had my stomach in a death grip was on its way out. The talk I'd had with my mom was good.

Annoying, sure.

But still good.

I may have been in a situation that had *suck* written all over it. But whining about it wouldn't help. It was time to ignore the big fat *what if?* that was hovering around my head everywhere I went. That door to dance awesomeness was still open.

It was time to either walk inside or close it for good.

▲▲▲▲▲▲▲▲▲

As soon as I got out of bed, I sent everyone a group text.

When Mom dropped me off at school, Kassie was already there on the sidewalk, hugging her arms to her. It was pretty cold, but I wasn't feeling the wind's bite. Everything from my neck down had gone numb from my decision. But it had to be done.

"I heard you all won last night," Kassie said, her face buried in the shadows of her hood.

"Um, yeah. Twenty-one to three. Do you know if the others are here?"

"Not yet."

"Okay, then before they show up—" A wispy cloud formed in front of my face as I exhaled. "What's the real reason you don't want to dance at that competition?"

She pulled her arms even tighter around her chest. "I already told you it doesn't matter."

"Yes, it does, Kass!" A few of the other students rubbernecked as they went by. I turned my head away, as if that'd do any good.

Kassie shivered. I bobbed on my toes a little closer to her, finally starting to feel the air trying to freeze my body. She let out a long breath. "You know how I told you about that solo my teachers gave Sarah? Well— that's sort of only half true."

I sniffed. My nose was numb, but the cold air was like a pair of icicles getting shoved up my nostrils. "So what happened?"

"My teacher did want Sarah to audition for it. And she actually did turn it down. But when it was my turn to dance for it—" Kassie lowered her head and her eyes disappeared in the shadows of her hoodie. "I choked. Like, epically."

"And they didn't give you another chance? That's so stupid."

"That's the thing. They did. When my dad finally convinced me to try, it was too late. They'd already made their decision."

She squeezed her shoulders together like she was trying to shrink. I'd never heard Kassie admit she was scared of anything. Especially dancing.

"I'll never forgive Sarah for taking it. Especially after

she promised me she wouldn't. And I know I messed up the steps, but it wasn't all my fault. They threw the choreography at me and expected me to just force it to fit. I tried it their way and it ruined my shot at nationals."

"But don't you want another chance? To show them you *can* dance?"

Kassie shook her head. "I can't dance in front of them. Not after I let those people beat me like that. Not after I let *her* beat me like that." Our eyes met for a second, but she looked away like she was humiliated.

A car pulled up and Carson jumped out. He walked over to us, his dad waving at us as he drove off. "Couldn't we have met next to a heater or something?"

"I figured you'd already be here."

"What's going on? Your text was a little—" Carson wrenched his face up in worried mode.

Kassie covered her face with her hands and groaned. "I don't know. Maybe this is stupid."

"What's stupid?" Carson asked.

"This plan. Me. This whole thing."

Carson held his hands up. "Whoa, hold on. Are you serious?"

"I don't *know*, Carson! Maybe?"

"Does that mean we're all going to dance instead?"

"No!" Kassie blurted out. "I still can't do that."

Carson let out a quick breath that sounded like a cross between a sigh and a growl. "Is this what the meeting was about? And are we finished? Because I'm dying out here." He blew into his hands like it was the coldest October in the history of Sunnydale.

"No," I said. "But I want to wait for Austin."

"Um, I wouldn't count on him showing up. Not after the other day."

I looked around for his mom's car, but Carson was right. "Okay. Fine. The reason I texted you guys—" I wiped my nose, pretending it was running. I just needed time to figure out how to say what I was there to say.

"Oh my gosh, Dillon, get on with it," Carson said.

"Sorry. Okay. The reason. I, um, got an email. And it said I made it into the top three for the scholarship."

Carson sucked in a gulp of air, clamping a hand over his mouth. Kassie didn't look as shocked. But she didn't look mad, either. Her eyes were huge, practically shaking in their sockets. I'd never seen her look so worried.

"So—what are you going to do?" she asked.

I chewed on my lip and immediately thought of what Mom had told me about gum. To pick the kind that makes you happiest. The only problem was, Kassie made me the happiest. Carson and Austin made me the happiest. But happy wasn't going to get me noticed by choreographers. Happy wasn't going to turn me into a real dancer.

So maybe happy wasn't what I needed.

"I'm . . ."

Fast, Dillon, I told myself. *Like a Band-Aid.*

"I'm gonna keep competing."

I stared at Kassie, waiting for her to say something. Anything. Then she looked out past the parking lot, her lips pressing into a hard line.

I wanted to reach out and touch her hand. To show her nothing had changed. That all I wanted was to get better. But I'd tried all that stuff before and it never seemed to work. "I swear I still want to be a part of the Dizzee—"

"Is that your final decision, then?" she asked. The icy look on her face made the wind around me feel like a warm breeze.

My heart lurched in my chest. Like it was sending out a Morse code message to my brain.

Don't. Say. Yes.

But I had to. And I did.

She snapped her hood back and turned to walk up the steps. Carson's face was still frozen in shock. But he managed to move. He raced up after her. "Kass, hold on!"

She stopped, listening to him. I couldn't hear everything, but I caught pieces of it.

". . . can't stand Sarah, but . . ."

". . . maybe he deserves . . ."

". . . still your friend . . ."

I made a quick mental note to hug Carson the next

time I had a chance. Kassie was going to turn around, nod, and say, *You're right. He does deserve it. And who cares if he goes to the Studio of Evil for three weeks? He'll still be our Kung Fu Kid when he comes back!*

And then I'd run up the stairs and hug her, too, and it wouldn't make me nervous because she'd be hugging me back. Then our eyes would lock and we'd stare at each other for a second and maybe we'd—

I blinked my eyes really fast. Kassie was staring at me like she was waiting for me to say something. Then I realized *she* had said something and I'd totally missed it.

I shook my head really fast. "I didn't hear what you said."

"I said you broke your promise! You had a choice and you chose Dance-Splosion." She spat out the name like it was a cussword.

Before I could say a thing, she was gone. Carson took a step after her, then stopped. He stomped down the steps, yanking his collar up over his neck. "I won't lie, Dillon. I'm like eighty percent mad you'd want to dance at the same place that Kassie hates. But I'm also like twenty percent proud of you."

"Gee. Thanks."

"So, is this it? Are you quitting the crew?"

"No! Not if I can help it, anyway. Maybe you could talk to her for me. I would, but I'm pretty sure it'd just make her madder."

"I'll try. But I'm not making any promises."

"Also, could you maybe talk to Austin? Tell him I still want to do the movie?"

Carson shrugged. "Again, no promises. I'll see you later, Dillon." He sped up the steps and headed inside.

The rest of the day, I was in a trance. My classes were a blur. Lunch was a fog.

But that Saturday without my crew—the first practice I'd ever missed—was the wake-up alarm I didn't want to hear.

And it wouldn't stop blaring the message *Rise and shine, Dillon Parker, loser of friends! You wanted to go solo, so get used to it!*

CARTER ACADUMMY IS SHARK FOOD!

That was the worst one.

Our homecoming game, the last one of the season, was on Thursday, and the cheerleaders had lined the halls with posters that said things like SQUASH THE SPARTANS! or TAKE A BITE OUT OF CARTER!

No wonder so many football players were mean. They had to walk around all day looking at bad one-liners.

Every time I saw myself in the bathroom mirror, I had this goofy, twisted-up expression on my face like it was hurting me to think. Maybe because it was. My decision was crawling around in my head, trying to find the perfect spot to fit.

I followed Kassie out of the cafeteria after lunch one

day, just to get a chance to see her. But then I felt like a stalker and turned around. Especially since she'd been heading to the bathroom at the time.

Coach Bear canceled Wednesday's practice to give everyone a chance to rest before the big game. Sarah decided since there was no way I'd ever get to play, I didn't need any rest. So she tacked on an extra private lesson. We ran through the entire routine three times without her screaming at me. The moves were actually starting to feel a lot better, but the more I did them, the more I missed my style.

Even if it *was* made-up.

"The finalist auditions are this Saturday and your spins still suck," Sarah said. "You're not spotting."

I threw my hands up in the air, frustrated. "Why do you always do that?"

"What?"

"Saying some dance word like I should know what it is. I wasn't born in a studio, you know."

Sarah planted her hands on her hips. "Who peed in your Cheerios this morning?"

I guessed that would've been me. Great.

I was Dillon Parker, the guy who peed in his own cereal.

"Hey, wake up," Sarah said, snapping her fingers. "I'm trying to teach you how to spot. Now watch."

She flew into a pirouette. It reminded me of Kassie.

Then she stopped, still as a statue, with no sign of dizziness.

"You can't just let momentum do all the work. You have to control it. Before you turn, focus on one point on the opposite wall. Then whip your head around to find the spot again. Try it."

I picked out a poster of a baseball player on the opposite side of the gym. I pulled my arms to the side and spun. Spotting wasn't too hard, but I still fell to the side and nearly landed on my face.

"Suck in your stomach while you turn. Keep your core tight."

That made it easier, but then I tripped over my own foot when I tried to stop.

"Did they let you get to green belt out of pity?" Sarah asked. She walked over to me and slammed her hand on my gut. "Keep this tight." Then she put her hands on my head and turned it so hard I thought she was trying to break my neck. "Turn this fast. Find your mark."

"Ow, geez. Do you have to be so rough?"

"I'm not—" She put her hands on either side of her face and growled. "It's just we have to get this right. I'm not going to let you get there and embarrass me in front of everyone."

"You mean you'll be watching me?"

"No. They're keeping this whole thing all secretive. Probably because it's the first year they've done it. But trust me, if you mess up, it'll come back to me. I know people, Dillon."

"Yeah, I bet. Don't worry, I won't give you a reason to go behind my back, too."

"What?" she said, looking genuinely shocked. "I didn't—"

"You can stop pretending, Sarah. Kassie told me everything."

Sarah jabbed a thumb into her chest. "*I'm* not the one who went behind her back, Dillon. I don't care what she told you!"

"Whatever, Sarah. You knew she wanted that solo more than anything. Were you expecting her to mess up the first time so you could jump in and steal it from her?"

"That wasn't me! That was—" Sarah's face was red. But not mad. This was shame. I'd felt enough of it to know. "I don't have to explain it to you."

I crossed my arms. My stubborn pose. I wasn't sure what I was waiting for her to say, really. I knew everything that had happened. And it wasn't like an apology would do any good, either.

"Back to first position," she said calmly, starting the music over. "You're not leaving here till you get this right."

My face was concrete. I needed her to see she couldn't boss me around. Even though I still sort of needed her to boss me around. But just until the contest was over.

"What happened between me and Kassie was—it was stupid. A mistake. I can't go back and fix it. So can we just keep working on your routine? Please?"

My concrete face melted a little. Maybe it wasn't my business anymore. To be honest, I wasn't even sure if Kassie was still my friend. I was still hers, though. So maybe it was only half my business.

We ran through it a couple of more times. I left with a pain in my neck and an ache deep in my chest.

The next day was Halloween. Half the school was decked out in too much hair gel and glitter. I headed to the gym for the homecoming game pep rally. The football team got to sit on one side while the cheerleaders entertained the entire middle school on the other for thirty minutes.

DeMarcus waved me over to the top of the bleachers. "Saved you a seat, man." He leaned over to say something but Coach Bear yelled into the microphone about Carter Academy. Our side of the gym exploded into a roar, sounding like a bunch of cavemen celebrating taking down a woolly mammoth—*GRRR! ARRGH! MUST BREAK OTHER TEAM!*

The arms in front of me settled back down. I squinted across the gym, trying to spot Kassie. But Troy's gigantic melon head blocked my view.

DeMarcus tapped me on the arm. He opened his mouth and paused, like his mind had gone blank. "Sorry," he said with a nervous laugh. "You ready for the game tonight?"

"Yeah. Ready to sit down for an hour and a half."

"I don't know, man. Coach put you in a couple of times during practice the other day. That's got to mean something."

I was pretty sure it didn't mean anything at all.

He cleared his throat. "So, your dance stuff. How's it going?"

"Well, it's . . . not, really."

"I thought you were training for some scholarship or something?"

"Oh. Yeah, I still am." I stared at my feet and one halfway-untied shoelace. "I thought you were talking about Kassie and Carson."

He shifted his weight, making it feel like the air tensed up beside me. "Nothing bad happened, did it? I mean between you guys?"

"It's complicated." I picked at a chipped spot on the bleacher seat right next to my leg.

DeMarcus buried his hands in his lap. "Okay, so . . . mind if I ask you a question?"

I shrugged.

"Did you happen to say anything to your friends? About me?"

"Um, maybe? Like you were nice probably. And dating Sarah—"

DeMarcus let out a loud sigh.

"What? Was I not supposed to?"

He kicked the seat in front of him. "Yeah. I mean no. Don't worry about it."

I wasn't worrying about it. My mind was a million miles away from DeMarcus and this side of the gym. I scanned the bleachers on the other side. Kassie. My eyes honed in on her like hoodie-seeking missiles. She was in the top row, between Carson and Austin. Her T-shirt had a big bar code printed above the words GENERIC HALLOWEEN COSTUME.

"You guys still talk and stuff, though, right?" DeMarcus asked.

"I don't know," I mumbled.

"But you're still friends, right? With all of them?"

"Look, if you want me to ask Kassie out for you, you can forget it." I don't know where the courage to back-talk the quarterback came from. I just hoped it'd send all my body's adrenaline to my legs when I had to somersault off the bleachers and start running for my life.

DeMarcus's face was one big nervous smile. I had no idea what he had to be uneasy about. One punch was all it would take from hands the size of his. He shook his head. "Never mind."

The muscles in my legs relaxed a little. Maybe I was safe.

After the pep rally, the gym emptied out into the hall-way. Imagining DeMarcus and Kassie sitting in Davie's Diner sharing an order of chili cheese fries turned the worry in my stomach to a full-blown intestinal panic attack.

Which might've been the chicken-fried steak they'd served us at lunch.

But I still wanted to see her.

I shoved my way toward a corner and peeked around it. Nothing but the backs of unfamiliar heads. But when I turned, she was coming down the hallway, talking to Carson and Austin.

She nearly ran right into me. She skidded to a stop and we both stood there staring at each other like the other one was a wild animal that might attack at any second. Carson grabbed Austin's arm and pulled. "Austin, didn't you want to show me something over here?"

"No," he said, but Carson had him lost in the crowd before he could argue any more.

There was a lot I wanted to say. Probably even more I *needed* to say. But all I could get out was a whispery "Sorry" as I lowered my head to walk around her.

"Hey, wait," she said. I did. My heart began kicking my chest bone so hard I was sure I'd have a bruise later on. Kassie took a deep breath. "Good luck. At the game."

The thudding behind my shirt slowed down. "Oh. Um, thanks." After a couple of awkward and silent seconds, I decided I wasn't ready to end the conversation yet. "So how have things been?" I asked.

She shrugged. "About the same." Students slid past us like we weren't even there. "How—how have you been?" Kassie asked.

I'd missed hearing her voice. The fact she still cared how I was made the hair on my arms stand up. "Okay, I guess."

Kassie had her hand pulled into her sleeve and was covering half her mouth with it. I wished she'd move it. Maybe I'd see her smile. "Top three are getting interviewed Saturday, right?"

"Yeah. Probably just embarrass myself."

She waved my comment off. "Nah. You're a great dancer. I know you think you're not, Dillon. But you are."

A smile forced its way onto my face, but it didn't last. "Look, Kass. I just want to say I hope we can—"

"I better go," she said really fast, looking away. "Bell's about to ring."

As she left, my entire body locked up. The words never came out of her mouth, but they slammed into my chest just the same.

Our friendship is over.

One minute we were dancing around a conversation almost like old times, and the next—*BAM!*—tackled by one silent sentence.

My worst nightmare had come to life right at the corner of the sixth- and seventh-grade hallways. But there was nothing I could do about it. And deep down, I wasn't that shocked.

I just wished I was more prepared for it.

Nobody ever said going for solo greatness would hurt so much.

Costco must've sold out of air horns.

Nearly every seat in the stands was filled with the butt of a die-hard football fan and every square inch of silence was drop-kicked out of the way by the ear-shattering honk of those stupid plastic cans of noise. If I hadn't been in such a sour mood, it probably wouldn't have bothered me that much.

We were beating Carter Academy pretty bad. Not that Coach Bear let us notice. When the clock was ticking down to the last few seconds, the Spartans called a time-out. I was holding down the bench with my rear end like I'd been doing all season. I had a spot picked out on the ground. A tiny little spider was trying to crawl up a blade of grass, but a couple of its legs were broken, so all it could do was flail around and fall back down. I knew exactly how it felt.

Just as I was about to lean down and help it up, a voice rang through the space between me and the sideline.

"Parker, now!" Coach Bear yelled.

"What?"

"I said you're up. Running back."

I laughed. "You're joking, right?"

"I don't get paid to joke, Parker. Now get out there and show me those moves."

I gave the spider one last look and wished it good luck. I walked over to Coach Bear, still thinking he was pranking me. But he grabbed the helmet out of my hands, slapped it over my head, and shoved me out onto the field. I walked over to where my team was huddled.

"What're you doin' out here?" Troy said, scratching the exposed part of his belly.

"Coach sent me in. Running back?" I wasn't sure why it came out as a question.

"Great," Bobby Fleagle huffed. "Last play of the game and I get replaced by Tighty Whitey." He shoved by me hard just as the other team was coming back to the field.

We huddled up and DeMarcus strung together a series of numbers and words that made absolutely no sense. He must've seen the look on my face, because he smiled and said, "Don't worry, Dillon. Just like in practice, okay?"

Everyone clapped and yelled, *"Break!"*

Just before everyone left the huddle, Troy grabbed my helmet and pulled me close. "Don't screw this up!"

We lined up. Before I remembered where I was supposed to stand, Troy snapped the ball. DeMarcus tossed it to Cody. My mind raced back to practice. *Protect your teammate!* I planted my feet, ready to block anyone who came my way. But just as Cody ran by, he shoved the ball into my hands. Why would he give me the ball? My mind raced for an answer. And then I remembered.

Fakeroo. Just like in practice.

I took off the opposite way. There were no cones to jump over. No tires to run through. But as long as I stayed away from the bright red uniforms, I'd be okay. One guy dove right toward me. I jumped over him, kicking one leg back and one leg forward, keeping my feet away from any grabby hands that tried to pull me back down.

Another guy came at me from the left. I pointed my toes, digging my feet into the dirt. He zipped right by me with a loud grunt.

Two more rushed in from the right. I spun. Core tight. Spot. Don't fall out of the turn. I took off, feeling fast. The crowd was screaming and I imagined myself onstage, finishing up a routine with the Dizzee Freekz, eardrums about to explode from the cheers Kassie, Carson, and I were getting. I imagined them smiling at me, wondering how I'd gone from ninja freestyle to real dancer so fast. I imagined Austin with one of those massive cameras that records in slow motion. I ran toward that end zone like my crew was there, waiting to take me back. I ran until my legs felt like they were about to buckle under me.

And then something crashed into my side, knocking the wind out of me.

I crumpled to the ground with a pair of gigantic meatheads on top of me. They practically had DESTROY DILLON plastered across their helmets.

I lay there holding the ball against my chest, feeling the pins and needles of excitement fade away as reality came crashing back down on top of me. There was no Kassie. There was no Carson. There was no Austin with his mega-camera. It was just me holding a leather ball in a giant rectangle of grass.

With a pair of airless lungs.

The referee blew his whistle. I looked up at the scoreboard. A bright red *BOOO* stared back at me. But then I realized it actually said 00:00.

The *BOOO* would've been more fitting, though.

Dillon, the Dumper of Friends.

Dillon, the Easily Tackled.

A hand reached down. DeMarcus. I peeled the football out of my chest as he pulled me to my feet.

"Nice run, man."

I had enough air in my lungs to squeeze out a soft laugh. "Whatever."

"You held on to the ball, didn't you? Ran the clock down. You should be proud."

We walked back to the sidelines with the rest of the team. As my chest reinflated, I actually did feel some pride soak into it, too. I had actually run a play. In a *game*. There wasn't a single blue shirt that had pulled that off this year.

After we lined up and congratulated the other team, Coach Bear gave us a quick postgame pep talk to say how proud he was of us. I got a few slaps on the back and everyone let loose a collective cheer, rivaling the air horns still blaring out their last bit of energy.

The sound wasn't bothering me as much anymore.

The players headed back toward the gate, ready to meet up with girlfriends, boyfriends, best friends.

I spotted Carson and Austin standing by the fence, throwing out their own congratulations to everyone. I pushed my way through a wall of football players. As soon as Austin saw me, the smile on his face disappeared.

"Hey," I said. "I didn't think you'd show up."

Carson shrugged. "We're still friends, Dillon. Even though you totally Beyoncé'd our Destiny's Child."

"He made me come," Austin said, getting a sharp elbow from Carson.

Carson rolled his eyes. "He came for you-know-who."

I'd figured as much. "Hey, about the other day—" I didn't even try to finish. The way Austin looked away, mumbling, made it clear talking to me was pretty low on his list. Probably ranked just below selling his camera and taking up yodeling as a hobby.

My eyes drifted up to the stands, hoping to find Kassie there somewhere.

"She's not here," Carson said. "We tried to get her to come, but . . ."

I nodded. Did I really expect her to be there?

Carson suddenly gasped at something over my shoulder. The scowl on Austin's face went from mild to *watch out!*

That could only mean DeMarcus. He propped his hands on the fence. "Hey, Dillon. These your friends?"

Maybe? I figured right then wasn't the best time to ask. "That's Carson. And that's Austin."

Carson waved. "You've, um, got a really good arm."

"Thanks. Little sore right now, though." DeMarcus laughed. A little louder than I would've expected him to. Sore arms weren't *that* funny.

Austin shrugged. "I saw you fumble it once."

I thought Carson was going to bite Austin's face off. Luckily, DeMarcus didn't hear him. A couple of other first stringers had walked up talking to him.

Carson leaned toward me, whispering. "My mom's taking us to Davie's Diner. Do you want to come?"

"Seriously?"

"I was thinking about texting Kassie. Maybe see if she'd come too so we can all talk. Like a crew meeting."

My stomach went all warm and stingy. Partly because the thought of seeing Kassie again was like a fiery ninja sword dancing ballroom in my gut. But also because at least one of my friends still wanted to hang out with me.

But I never had time to answer.

"*There* you are," a silky-smooth voice butted in. Sarah. She slid in next to me, wrapping her arms around De-Marcus's gigantic shoulder pads. "Ready to go? Everyone's waiting."

He tugged at his jersey collar and Sarah let go of him.

"Hello, Sarah!" Austin said. Way too loud. He had to have noticed, because his face went all blotchy red.

"I was just saying hi to Dillon's friends," DeMarcus said. "The dancers."

"Is that what they call themselves?" Sarah said with a smirk. Carson shot her a tight-lipped scowl. She rolled her eyes. "Just a joke. Calm down."

"Whatever." Carson let out a loud sigh and looked at me. "So, the diner?"

Austin punched his arm. "You invited him?"

"Yes, I invited him," Carson said, rubbing his arm. "You in, Dillon?"

"Um, no. He's not in," Sarah said.

"Excuse me, but you don't get to decide for him. He can make up his own mind."

I cleared my throat. "Maybe I—"

"Shut up, Dillon, you're coming with us," Carson said, still glaring at Sarah.

"Dude, you didn't even ask me first!" Austin hissed.

Sarah beamed an eyelash-fluttering smile at DeMarcus. "Babe, why don't you go find the others. I'll catch up."

DeMarcus looked at me, then back to Sarah. He sighed, said goodbye, and disappeared into the sea of jerseys and helmets. Sarah grabbed my arm and pulled me away from the fence.

"I swear I'm not in the crew anymore. Kassie—she kicked me out. You can ask them."

Her jaw tensed. "You need to remember what I said about her reputation."

"But—"

"No. Now, you need me more than I need you. So you either listen to your teacher or this is finished. I'll make one call and tell them you got caught shoplifting or something and they'll replace you faster than you can say *grand jeté*."

Sarah stared me down. I slung my helmet against my leg. Tired. But not from running. Because I'd barely even done any. No, what had me feeling like I could collapse were all the looks. All the constant orders. All the trying to be someone different.

"Look," she said. "I know I'm still being tough. But that's because you really have gotten better. I think you've got a good chance at this."

I shook my head. She might've thought so. I wasn't so sure.

"And also because, believe it or not—" She looked me up and down. "Me and you are a lot alike."

If I had any laugh inside me, I would've let it out right then.

"We both know what it takes to get to the top. We both know that sometimes you have to ignore the people you care about to get there. Am I right?"

I looked toward the fence. Carson and Austin were watching like they were witnessing a ten-car pileup. I was crashing in slow motion and I was caught in that in-between moment where I had to either stay in the car and get smashed into a million pieces or fling my seatbelt off and dive-roll out.

Behind them, my parents were weaving down the bleachers, shaking hands and saying hi to people they knew. If this were a movie, I'd toss my helmet on the ground and stomp off toward the fence. Maybe beg my way back onto the crew. *The Return of the Kung Fu Kid.*

But this wasn't a movie.

This was real life. And I was stuck right in the middle of it. So what'd I do?

Practically the opposite of all of that. I mustered up the best smile I could, shot it toward Carson and Austin . . .

And walked away.

20

▲▲▲▲▲▲▲▲▲

On the way to Dance-Splosion that Saturday, Sarah kept texting me in all caps to not forget all the stuff she'd told me to remember.

If I hadn't needed my phone, I would've tossed it out the window.

Even through the phone she couldn't stop yelling at me.

We pulled into the parking lot and I stared up at the building. This time it didn't look as huge. A little less intimidating.

But my stomach still decided to take a nosedive down toward my feet.

I tightened my grip around the straps of my duffel bag. My mom put her hand on my back and gave my shoulder a little squeeze.

But Dad? Ever since our conversation he'd been all closed off. I couldn't tell if he was mad at me for back-talking him or what. Every now and then, though, I'd catch him and Mom whispering to each other. And not the gushy my-parents-are-totally-in-love type of whispering, either.

Inside Dance-Splosion, a big-screen TV had their commercials playing on loop. *Dance-Splosion . . . where real dancers are made.* After the third one, Dad let out an uncomfortable-sounding sigh-grumble. "Why can't I just wait in the van?"

Mom smacked his arm and put on a friendly smile for the girl at the front desk. It was a different girl than before. "Hello, we're here for the scholarship candidates' audition. Dillon Parker. From Sunnydale. He's in the top three."

"She's got it, Mom, thanks," I said.

The girl wrote something down on a piece of paper. "Just follow the hall to auditorium three. Good luck today, Dillon."

I lit the room up with a quick blush and followed my parents past the desk. We went by one room with an all-guy group full of leg muscles that were about to pop through their tights. Dad's jaw dropped and I just knew he was going to make some comment about all that strength going to waste or something. But he never did. He just mouthed *Wow* and kept on walking.

We stopped outside the auditorium doors. Mom tried to smoosh my hair down and tuck in my shirt.

"Mom, stop. I'm gonna be changing into my dance uniform in a minute anyway."

"You need to make a good first impression, sweetie," she said, turning me around, stuffing as she went. She gave me a quick kiss, smeared away the lipstick with her thumb, and headed up the stairs, following the sign that pointed them toward the "viewing room."

As soon as they were gone, I dug my shirt out of my sweat pants and took a deep breath. *This is it*, I thought. *What it's all been for.*

I walked inside. The room was just like the photo on the website: the pale blue walls were lined with those stretching bars and the floors were polished wood. The knot in my stomach loosened just a bit.

On the far side, two other dancers were warming up. To the right was a table where a man and a woman were sitting, both with a stack of papers in front of them. Something to my left caught my eye and I looked up. A large window showed the viewing room, where people could sit and watch. My mom was pointing frantically, probably at my loose shirttail, and getting a few laughs and looks from the other parents.

I didn't see a spot where I could change, so I made my way up to the table. The man—a bald guy with nerd glasses—was busy typing something on his phone, but the woman, who had super-short hair and a friendly face, welcomed me with a smile.

"Hi. I'm Dillon. I'm here for the audition?"

"We're just about to begin," Mrs. Smiley said.

"Do you know what music I'll be dancing to?"

"All three contestants will be dancing to the same music," Mrs. Smiley said. "You can take a seat in the back while we get ready, okay?" She smiled and pointed to the far corner.

I found a seat next to the two other dancers. I pushed my legs out straight to warm up, glancing at my competition. A guy who looked like he belonged in an Axe Body Spray commercial and a skinny girl with wavy brown hair. Her legs were as long as my entire body and as thin as my arms. She looked around my age, but probably a foot taller. Her feet were together, pulled all the way toward her. She grabbed her ankles and butterflied her knees. I glanced down at her tights. There was a hole in one of the knees and the blue color was all faded everywhere else.

"Hi," she said. I jerked my eyes away, but it was too late. She'd already seen me staring. "My name's Avery. Broadway."

"Cool last name."

Avery laughed. "No, I *dance* Broadway. My last name's Yates."

"Oh. My name's Dillon. I dance, um . . ."

I didn't want to say it. Not while I was sitting in the middle of a dance studio. No, *the* studio. Saying the words *ninja freestyle* would probably get me thrown out. Besides, that part of me was gone.

I wasn't the Kung Fu Kid anymore.

"You don't know your style?" the guy next to us said. He'd had his legs stretched out in front of him with his head buried in his knees since I'd sat down. I thought he'd fallen asleep like that.

"I know my style. It's just going through some . . . changes."

"What does that even mean?" he asked, with his head all smothered in a cocky grin.

It means I don't like your face, jerk. I wanted to say that. But I didn't. The studio probably had rules against things like that.

Mrs. Smiley stood and walked around the table.

"Hello, everyone. First of all I want to congratulate you all for making it this far. My name is Jackie. I'm a senior faculty member here at Dance-Splosion. I teach contemporary and ballet." She turned toward Mr. Baldy. "And this is Robert. Another one of our wonderful contemporary instructors. He's usually not this shy." He rolled his eyes, but she didn't seem to care.

"We'll begin by asking you some questions about your dance history. There are no wrong answers—we're just wanting to get to know you. Afterward you'll be performing your improvised solo. Again, don't worry about getting it wrong. We're only looking for your interpretation. Are there any questions?"

We all stayed quiet.

"All right. We'll be conducting the auditions in alphabetical order."

I straightened up. Avery was a *Y* and I was a *P*. We had the end of the alphabet pretty much taken care of. Going last was the ideal spot. I pulled my sweats down over my football pants, glancing at Mr. Stretchy. That's when I spotted the name on his equipment bag: Kenton Whittenbarger.

The jerk was a *W*.

"Dillon?" Mrs. Smiley said. "You'll be up first."

I should've told them my name was Dillon Zachary. Or something cool like Dillon Zeus. I took a deep breath and walked to the table.

"So, Dillon, how long have you been dancing?" Mrs. Smiley asked, sitting down.

"For about a year and a half. But it feels like a lot longer."

She laughed. But not Mr. Baldy. He looked as amused as an old woman at a rap concert.

"That's good," she said. "You seem like you enjoy it."

"Yes, ma'am, I do." Manners. Nailed it.

"Where did you learn to dance?"

Saying *I never did, that's why I'm here, duh,* probably

wouldn't have been smart. So I stuck to the safe answer.

"I guess I just taught myself. From watching other dancers and stuff. Oh, and from when I took karate."

Mr. Baldy's head snapped up. "Karate?"

"Um, yes, sir. Some of my moves are—*were*—sort of inspired by it when I took it." Just saying that in front of them sounded stupid.

"Interesting," he said, writing something down. But the way he said it made me wish I could take it back.

"So no formal training, then?" Mrs. Smiley asked.

"Um, no, ma'am. Sorry."

"No, don't be sorry, Dillon." She made a quick note, then looked back up at me. "What made you decide to send in a video?"

I knew they'd bring it up eventually. "Yeah, about that. I'm sorry for sending that in. I would've made another one, but the deadline was almost over." My face felt like it was about to catch on fire.

Mrs. Smiley held up her hands. "No, no, no—I wasn't asking about that. And wardrobe malfunctions happen more than you'd think, trust me." She put her hands down. "I just wanted to know why you entered the competition."

My lungs froze. Telling them I'd entered because my dance crew leader wanted me to sabotage their competition was probably a bad idea. But I wasn't there for that anymore. A long sigh escaped through my lips. "For the longest time, I've been trying to get better. But I never had anyone who would teach me. Then I saw your website with the contest announcement and thought—I should just go for it. This is where real dancers are made, right?"

"Well, the first thing you'll need to learn is what a real dancer performs in." Mr. Baldy's eyes were scanning a page in front of him. "Do you not have any dance tights?"

I looked down at my football pants. One of the knees had a little tear in it. Perfect. Stains, holes, rips . . . I was about to show my stuff in front of the most prestigious dance academy and I'd come in looking like a hobo.

"No. Not yet. I usually just dance in jeans."

"We usually advise against that. Jeans don't allow for a lot of movement," Mrs. Smiley said.

"Yes, ma'am, I figured that out. But my crew said I needed to wear them."

"Oh, you're on a crew?"

A lump in my throat instantly swelled to the size of a football. Yeah, I was on a crew. Once. "Not anymore. I just got too—busy. Football and stuff."

"I understand," Mrs. Smiley said. "And what style of dance do you perform?"

"It's, um—contemporary."

Mrs. Smiley leaned back in her chair. "Well, we look forward to seeing what you can do, Dillon. Are you ready to get started?"

"Yes, ma'am."

"Okay. When we cue the music, you can begin."

21

▲▲▲▲▲▲▲▲▲

I walked to the middle of the room and did a quick checklist.

No kicks. No punches. No jumping. No fake sword-fighting.

Basically most of what my body was used to. I slid my feet into first position, mentally running through my routine while I waited.

Mrs. Smiley motioned to a girl who looked young enough to possibly be a Dance-Splosion student. She pushed a button on a small iPod dock. A wave of music I'd never heard before filled the room. But at least it was classical just like Sarah had said.

I closed my eyes and let my body do its thing.

I let every note, every melody, pour into my brain.

The song soaked into my muscles and bones, all the way down to the tips of my fingers and toes. With one last big inhale, I was off.

Sissonne, step, step, spin.

Core tight, spot. Land.

I didn't fall. My body rocked to the side a little, but I stayed on my feet.

Next, I leaped forward, forcing my toes down as hard as I could. A reach to the left, swing the arms right. I realized my fists were clenched. I shook them loose, playing it off like I was flapping my arms like wings. Or maybe doing jazz hands.

My arms wanted to fly out into a barrage of chops and slices so bad! But those were on the Do Not Perform list. And to make things worse, I'd forgotten the next move. I was supposed to get from a long reach to the right to me on the floor reaching to the left.

So instead, I swiped my arms through the air. Graceful, feathery, relaxed. Just like Sarah had taught me.

I rolled to the floor, making sure my body was as stiff as a board. It felt terrible. Like I'd been dipped in glue and I couldn't bend.

With a quick hop, I was back on my feet. And totally lost. The music was different. My moves were different. I had to dance my guts out for those judges, but I couldn't let go like I usually did. Sarah wasn't kidding when she said there were rules to dance. But with all the pressure of the competition running through my veins, my body just didn't want to obey them.

I'd barely done anything and I was already out of breath. But if I was gonna win this thing, I had to give every ounce of energy I could. I had to dance so hard I'd collapse into a puddle of dance awesomeness at the end.

Then the music stopped.

Not ended—stopped. As in someone cut it off.

I turned to look at the judges, sweat flying off the end of my nose.

"Dillon, you said you were learning some new moves?" Mrs. Smiley said.

"Yeah. I mean, yes. I'm still trying to get them right, but I'm a hard worker. I swear."

"I'm sure you are. But what about the dancing I saw in your video?"

I shook my head. "I don't do that style anymore. I promise."

"That's a shame. What'd you call it when you *did* dance it?"

There was no getting around it. I had to say it. "I called it ninja freestyle."

Someone snorted behind me. The *W* with the jerky face.

"But I've been learning some new moves. Like spins and retirés and lots more."

Mrs. Smiley leaned over to Mr. Baldy, whispering

behind her hand. Whatever she was saying, he didn't seem to be a big fan of it. After he huffed out an annoyed "Fine," she turned to me. "Do you think you could show us some of that? The ninja freestyle? I was intrigued by your style when I saw your video. It's why I made you my top pick as one of the finalists."

Every inch of my body screamed, *YES! Ninja-freestyle your way into solo greatness RIGHT NOW!* I glanced behind me at Avery and Kenton. I'd never seen them dance, but I would've bet their technique didn't have any punches and kicks.

I remembered what Sarah had told me. About control and discipline and rules. About lines and grace and weightlessness. About how I had none of that when I was dancing the way I'd taught myself.

And especially about how she'd find out what happened here, because she had spies or minions or something.

"I don't dance like that anymore."

The words felt sourer than an entire mouthful of Warheads. But I was there to win. I was there to become a real dancer.

Mrs. Smiley leaned forward. "I really wish you'd reconsider."

If that room had been a stage, every spotlight would've been pointing at me as they waited for an answer. A word, a move—*anything!*

"I can't," I said. "I'm sorry."

Mr. Baldy mustered up a smile that looked like it was hurting his face. "Thank you, Dillon. We've seen enough."

I walked to the back of the room and slid down the wall, feeling about as crummy as the football locker room floor. Avery was picking at the frayed edge of her ballet slippers. Her eyes were glued to the judges. They were whispering, hiding their mouths with their hands. I stretched my neck forward, trying to hear them.

"Trust me, you don't want to know what they're saying," Kenton said, flipping his surfer hair out of his eyes.

"You don't have to be mean," Avery said.

"Just being honest."

I picked up my sweats and laid them across the butchered knees of my football pants. "It's not the music I'm used to. Plus the floors in there are way more slippery than—"

He smirked. "You don't have to make excuses."

"I'm not!" I snapped, my face feeling hot. I looked at the judges, but they were still talking.

Kenton put his hands up in *Calm down, dude* mode. "Look, you're obviously not as trained and it shows."

I didn't need some turd with expensive tights to tell me that. Right as I opened my mouth, hoping a really good comeback would pop out, the iPod girl walked over.

"They'd like to see you, Kenton."

He tossed his earbuds in his bag and jumped to his feet. "Might want to take some notes."

Kenton followed the girl to the middle of the room. His feet snapped to first position. Even his feet looked jerky. Who knew, maybe I'd get lucky and he'd sprain a leg. Maybe he'd have his own blowout and get kicked out of the studio for showing everyone his crack.

I shoved the thoughts away. Dancers probably didn't go around wishing horrible things to happen to other dancers. So I sat there just listening to him pop off his answers like he'd been practicing them for weeks. Mind cleared. No wishing.

But if he did happen to face-plant halfway through his routine, I wouldn't complain.

"Don't listen to him," Avery said, her mouth lifting into a sympathetic smile. "He's just trying to get into your head is all."

I wondered why she was so nice. Compared to Sarah and Kenton, she was a Disney princess. Too bad I couldn't have *her* tutor me all year.

After Kenton answered all the judges' questions, the music started and he began his solo. I should've known by his shoes that he was a ballet dancer. They looked a lot like Sarah's except they were black. As soon as he moved, a heavy weight grew in my stomach.

He was good.

And his legs were a pair of springs.

The guy did a double spin in the air and landed without even making a single sound. Every leap was a mile long. In fact, most of his moves were some sort of jumping. He didn't do a whole lot of other stuff. At least I had rolled to the ground once.

After a couple of minutes, the music stopped, just like it had with mine. I perked up. Mr. Baldy was giving him a halfhearted thanks while shuffling through a stack of papers. Maybe there was hope after all. Maybe nobody got through an entire routine.

Kenton walked toward the back of the room and sat down, popping his earbuds in. He scowled at the two of us. "What?"

Avery shrugged and looked at me, giggling. I tried not to, but I couldn't help it. I smiled back.

"At least I didn't show up in a bunch of hand-me-down junk," Kenton grumbled.

The smile on Avery's face disappeared. "It's not hand-me-down—"

"Just regular junk, then. Okay, I get it."

Avery hugged her legs against her chest. She sat there, eyes glued to the floor, until iPod Girl walked over.

"Avery Yates? You're up."

When she stood, a loose thread from her legging got stuck under her foot. She took a step and the top of it split open.

"Whoa, wait," I said, but as I reached forward, Kenton pushed my hand back.

Avery glanced over her shoulder, the hurt from Kenton's last comment still fresh on her face. "What?"

Kenton gave his head a quick shake. I knew why he

wouldn't want me to say anything, but that wasn't my style. Then again, it wasn't like my style had been doing me a lot of good lately.

You're here to win. Even if that means stepping on a few toes, I thought. *And letting your competition trip over their own.*

"Just . . . good luck."

"Thanks." She smiled and found her spot in front of the judges, the loose legging thread trailing behind her.

I'd sent her off to dance with a legging that was primed for malfunction. I wasn't just stepping on toes. I was kicking shins and taking out kneecaps, too. I sank back against the wall, my insides cramping up.

Her audition questions were the same as everyone else's. I learned she'd been dancing since she was four. She'd gone to a studio in Illinois, but recently her family had had to move down to Georgia. She'd been looking for an academy, but couldn't find one that her dad could—

She stopped. She looked down at her shoes. So did I.

And that's when I got it. Her tights with the tiny rip in the knee. Her leggings with the string hanging out. Her shoes with the edges all scuffed up. Maybe she wasn't going for the *I'm an angry punk girl dancer* look. Maybe that's all she had. A bunch of clothes that she'd nearly danced into threads.

If there was anyone who knew how clothes could

sabotage a routine, it was me. I leaned forward, trying to get her attention.

Look behind your foot. Just turn around and look behind your stupid foot! I chanted it over and over in my head. Because I couldn't bring myself to actually say anything. Not when I knew she was one of the dancers standing between me and Dance-Splosion.

Mrs. Smiley asked if she was ready to dance. Avery said she was, and a few seconds later the music began. It was the same music I'd already heard twice, but for some reason it sounded a million times sadder than before. Avery floated around the floor, reaching toward the judges, quick-stepping into a spin, leaping through the air and landing into a roll. She was incredible. The thread whipped around behind her and for a while I thought it might stay out of her way.

But I was wrong.

Avery planted her feet. The end of the thread was caught under her left foot. She raised her arms to the side. I knew exactly what move she was going for. The sissonne. Which would've been easy enough, except that—

"Aaah!"

She fell to the side as soon as she lifted her knee. Her legging tore all the way down to her ankle, falling open like a banana peel. She hit the ground hard.

Kassie.

For a split second, that's all my brain would register. Kassie's solo. Maybe in this same room. When she choked. Maybe in that same spot.

Avery looked back at me. I gave her a wide-eyed nod to say *Just keep going!* She couldn't quit. She was too good.

But her eyes, jumping from one person to the next like she expected one of us to start pointing and laughing, filled with tears. She darted out of the room with one legging trailing behind her.

The music stopped and Mr. Baldy leaned over, whispering something to Mrs. Smiley. Kenton had his earbuds out and had this half smile plastered on his face like he couldn't believe what'd just happened. He gave me an up-and-down glance. "Looks like it's down to the two of us, then," he said, and went back to his music.

I should've been happy. No, thrilled. Half of my main competition had just thrown away their spot, and I was one step closer to winning that scholarship.

So why did I feel so bad?

22

▲▲▲▲▲▲▲▲▲

The car ride home was quiet.

I felt like I was going to a funeral. But the only thing that had died was my chance of winning that scholarship. My phone buzzed in my bag as Dad merged onto the interstate.

Sarah: y didn't u text me???

Great. I was hoping she'd wait until Monday before she interrogated me. My fingers flew over the letters faster than my brain could figure out what I should say.

Me: maybe bc I was busy trying not to look like an idiot.

There was a pause and I immediately wished I hadn't texted her that. Now she'd think I'd bombed the routine. Worse than I actually did, anyway. So I sent her another text.

Me: but i think i did ok. the judges were just tough.
Sarah: what did the judges say? did they like the choreo?
Me: they stopped me halfway through and asked for my ninja freestyle.

I wanted to hit send so bad I could taste it. Sarah would read it and probably explode. I'd be able to look out the van window and see where she was by the gigantic mushroom cloud forming in the sky. But my chances of winning would go up in smoke along with her.

So I deleted it and just sent: *yes*.

I threw myself back against the backseat.

Monday morning, there was no high-fiving. No hugs. No Sarah congratulating me for not getting kicked out of the contest for busting out some of my old moves. She just paused for a second with her Barbie marching band and stared off over my head, saying, "You still need work. Just because you're in the top three doesn't mean we're safe."

She walked off. I kicked the air behind her and heard something pop. My first thought was that I'd ripped my jeans. Great. Tighty Whitey strikes again. I backed up against the lockers and slid my hand behind me to check. All clear. When I turned to walk away, an eighth-grade girl was staring at me with her eyebrows perched as high up on her forehead as they could possibly get. She blew a bubble.

Pop!

I smiled, but she just rolled her eyes and left.

At lunch, I took the long route to the football table. I didn't care if it was technically spying, I had to see my friends. I'd just sneak by. Just a quick look. I followed a pair of girls walking near the table, keeping close and as hidden as possible. I craned my neck, looking over their shoulders and—

SCREEECH!

The earsplitting squeak my shoes made shot through the cafeteria like an arrow. Kassie and Carson looked up at me. And so did the four new faces, including the one sitting in my old seat. Austin, though? He just stared straight ahead, shoving one fry after another into his mouth.

My heart churned out a techno beat, making my entire body shake. This was it. I'd been replaced. My own best friends had found new people.

The corners of Kassie's mouth pulled back into a weird sort of awkward smile. The kind you give cousins you don't really know. The type you save for school pictures.

"Um, hey. How's it going?" I inched closer to my seat.

Since they hadn't chased me off yet, I thought I'd sit down. Maybe the guy with the spiky hair and black-rimmed glasses would take a hint and scram.

I balanced on the tips of my toes, waiting for Kassie to reply. And when she did—it was a shrug.

A *shrug*. A bolt of white-hot fear zigzagged through my body. I tried to keep myself from hyperventilating, which is hard to do when you've just witnessed yourself being kicked out of the only place you've ever fit in. I said the first thing that popped into my head. "I miss you."

Captain Spiky Hair grinned and looked at Kassie. Her eyes fell to the table. I couldn't be sure but it looked like her face was a little pinker than it had been a few seconds earlier. Great. First real words I say to Kassie in forever and all I manage to do is embarrass her.

I quickly added, "All of you, I mean. Hanging out. And stuff." *And stuff.* Brilliant. They'd take me back for sure now. Because I missed all the *and stuff* and stuff.

"We missed you, too, Dillon," Carson said. Did he say *missed*? As in, *We* used *to miss you, Dillon. But not anymore because we have new besties with colorful shirts and spiky hair.*

Austin nodded toward Captain Spiky Hair. "That's Patrick. He's a filmmaker, too."

"Whassup?" Patrick said. "We're making a zombie movie for the film festival this summer. It's gonna be disgusting, bro."

I nearly dropped my tray. "*Our* zombie movie?"

"It's *my* zombie movie, Dillon," Austin said. "I'm the one who wrote it."

"Okay, but—am I still gonna be in it?"

"Well . . ." Austin scratched his forehead.

Before he could say anything else, Patrick jumped in. "Movie's already been recast, bro. Austin said you already had things going on this summer. Too bad. But maybe we could use you as an extra." He stuck his thumb out toward the three other new kids. The ones stuck on the end of the table, who'd been quiet the whole time. The extras. The blue shirts of the movie world.

I glared at Patrick through the little spews of steam rising off the meat loaf. For a second I imagined dumping every bit of it on his head. More than a lot of me was hoping that Kassie and Carson would speak up. I only waited for like five seconds, but it felt like forever. Like when the judges on all the dance competition shows get ready to tell everyone who the winner is and they pause. And stare. And wait. And then they say, "You made it to the next round!" and everyone screams and cheers and there's crying, but it's the good kind.

That. Except the total opposite.

I fake-smiled through a thick layer of pain. "Fine. I gotta go. Good seeing you."

I found a seat at a random table. Far away from Kassie, Carson, and Austin and far away from Sarah and the football team. I wanted to be alone. I wanted to be sad. I wanted to sit there and pout and stew in my own feel-awfulness. For a while I thought I'd done this to myself. That it was me who had kicked my friends to the side. That it was me who had given up my crew for solo greatness.

But I wouldn't have even been there if my own crew hadn't pressured me into it. They were the ones who'd shoved me into a corner where I didn't fit. And somewhere along the way—just when I was finding out where I might belong—they'd replaced me. With a spiky-haired hipster and a handful of extras.

After school, I made my way to the gym. Sarah wasn't there, so I sat down and spent the first ten minutes stretching and watching videos.

I replayed every single one Austin had put up on our—*their*—YouTube channel. There was even a new one. The routine looked pretty much the same, but a few spots had been changed to work with two people instead of three.

One less fake dancer made the dance look twice as good.

On the new video, I could hear Austin arguing with Patrick about zooming in or tilting the camera. The only reason I knew it was Patrick was because he'd end nearly every sentence with *bro*. Well, that and his voice made me want to tear off my ears.

My nickname was never mentioned. Maybe Patrick had convinced Austin to edit me out. Or maybe it'd been Austin's idea. I'd never know. So I just watched them practice and get better. Every video had some comments. Most were the usual junk, but I noticed a couple asking where the Kung Fu Kid was. Carson responded to both: "Taking a break for now."

More like forever.

My phone buzzed.

Sarah: u better b practicing. i can't make it 2day. girl stuff.

Sarah or no Sarah, I needed to practice. The competition was Saturday and I was still falling out of my turns a little. I pulled up the snorefest of a song I'd been practicing to and stood up. I took a deep breath and pushed off the ground. Toes like knife points.

Two stiff-legged steps and into a retiré to begin my pirouette. I added in an extra spin, spotting both times.

My body felt weird. The technique was getting there. But it was like I was dancing in a shell. Just riding along while someone else pushed me around the floor.

I ended my turn, reaching out to the left, then to the right. My left leg flew up behind me. My next move was to bring it back down and roll to the floor.

But I didn't.

I couldn't.

My body was refusing.

So I swung my leg forward into a teeth-shattering front kick. I pulled two imaginary swords from my belt, spinning across the room. Punches, kicks, uppercuts. Every move that'd been bottled up inside me for weeks was tearing down the wall of technique I'd been using to hold it back.

I was a ninja, slicing my way through hordes of monsters, saving the universe from evil.

And I couldn't stop.

When the music faded out, I stood there, sweat dripping off my nose.

My chest ached from breathing so hard.

Something was wrong. Ninja freestyle wasn't real. It wasn't dancing.

Real dancers danced real styles.

But that didn't explain why it still felt so good to do.

That evening, I was in the middle of my algebra homework when I got another text from Sarah.

Sarah: u practice like u were supposed 2?

Practice? Yes. Like I was supposed to? Not exactly.

Me: Yes.
Sarah: good. don't make plans 4 friday.
Me: Why?

I sank into my chair. Friday was an in-service day. A free day. The last thing I wanted was another day being stuck with her.

Sarah: ur coming to the movies with us.
Me: You mean like a date?
Sarah: gross. no. it's the last day b4 the contest. i don't want u 2 do anything stupid.

"Like going to the movies with you?" I said to the screen.

Not like I had a choice. But maybe getting out would be good. Probably better than being glued to my desk, fantasizing about Patrick getting accidentally knocked into a concussion by Kassie.

23

▲▲▲▲▲▲▲▲▲

The smell of over-buttered popcorn and old carpet hit me as soon as I walked inside the theater.

"You invited Tighty Whitey?" Bobby said, snarling at me as I got close.

"I also invited you," Sarah said, returning the sass. The two Barbies laughed in unison.

"So, what're we seein'?" Troy asked.

Sarah turned to DeMarcus. "What did you have in mind, Mr. Quarterback?" She put her arms around his neck.

"Oh, um, I don't know." He pulled her hands off him. "What did you all want to see?"

Sarah glared at him for a second, like she couldn't believe he didn't instantly dip her and plant a big wet one on her lips. DeMarcus shoved his hands in his pockets.

Troy held his hands up in front of him. "Better not be a chick flick."

"Yeah," Bobby said. "Don't want Troy to turn gay on us." He honked out a laugh that sounded like a cross between a goose and a burp.

"Shut up, Bobby. I'm not the one who got replaced by Tighty Whitey last game."

"Whatever," Bobby mumbled. "He ain't got half the moves I do." He walked off toward the concession counter with Red-Haired Barbie.

My eyes landed on the Dance Dance Revolution game at the mini-arcade and my stomach instantly knotted up. I pulled out a wad of quarters from my pocket. "So, um, anyone wanna play air hockey?"

"What are you, like five years old?" Black-Haired Barbie asked.

"Yeah, I'll play," DeMarcus said.

I followed him over to the table and popped the four coins into the change slot. The surface poofed out a burst of air and the tiny plastic disc hovered across the playing field.

"Um, you wanna go first?" I asked.

"It's all you, man," DeMarcus said, his eyes skipping over to where Sarah was standing.

I aimed and struck. The ear-popping CLACKs echoed through the theater as the disc ricocheted around the table. Within a few seconds, DeMarcus scored. I replaced the disc on the table and aimed again.

CLACK!

"It was fun finally getting to play this year," I said.

CLACK!

"Mm-hm."

CLACK!

"The first string seems pretty cool."

CLACK!

"Yeah. Most of them."

CLACK!

"I sort of miss hanging out with my friends, though."

CLACK!

Just a nod.

CLACK!

"Especially—" *Shut up, Dillon, shut up, Dillon, don't say her name, Dillon, it'll just make you feel like crawling into a corner and dying.* "Austin and Carson."

BEEP!

I scored. DeMarcus set the disc back on the table, scooting it to where he wanted it to rest, and paused. He stood there, his hands pressed on the edge of the game, staring at the bright blue surface. Finally, he took a deep breath. "This is stupid."

"We don't have to keep playing if you don't want to."

"No, it's not that." He looked over at Sarah. "It's her. Or more like *us*, I guess."

I tried to look surprised, but I wasn't. I'd figured out he was over Sarah a while ago. "Why don't you just break up with her?"

A soft laugh broke away from him. "Yeah, right. You know what would happen to my reputation if I did that, man?"

I didn't. Mostly because I'd never had a reputation other than Tighty Whitey. "You know, if you ever need to talk or something . . ." My voice trailed off, having no idea what to say next. Not like I was some girlfriend-advice-giving expert.

He pulled off his jacket, his arms flexing under his shirt. "What's there to talk about?"

"The fact that you actually like someone else?"

He let out a weak laugh. "You don't know the half of it. You're right, though. I do like someone else."

I tossed my paddle back on the table. The last thing I wanted to do was let him think I was okay with him falling in love with Kassie. But I also knew how hanging around Sarah could slowly suck the life out of a person. "I guess I don't blame you really. She is pretty cool."

His eyes hit mine for a second, like he was going to say something. But he didn't. I slid my paddle back and forth on the table a few times before he finally did speak. "It's tough, man. I can't even say anything about it. Not while I'm stuck. With them."

We stood there a few seconds, silent. There wasn't anything I could say, really. And if there was, I wasn't sure we were good enough friends for me to offer advice to the guy.

"You want to play a different game?" he finally asked.

"Okay." I glanced around the arcade, but DeMarcus was already heading over to Vocal Hero.

When I got over there, he was stuffing the quarters into the coin slots. I'd played the game a lot with Austin. On two-player mode, you could choose either guitar or vocals. We'd always end up arguing who got to play the guitar, because neither one of us ever wanted to sing.

I didn't want to seem like a whiner in front of him, so I said, "I'll take vocals, I guess."

DeMarcus snatched up the microphone. "You can have them next round. This one's all mine." His eyes reflected the explosions of color blasting from the screen.

The guy actually *wanted* the vocals. The star quarterback with huge biceps, and I felt sorry for him. He was about to make a total fool of himself in front of everyone. "What song do you want?"

"I don't care. You pick."

So I did. I scrolled through the list and selected my favorite. The song that had started my entire trip.

"We Will Rock You" by Queen.

The animated people on the screen bobbed their heads to the beat. Luckily, the guitar didn't come in until later. Which was good because I didn't want to be the one who got us booed off the imaginary stage. DeMarcus put both hands on the mike as the lyrics inched closer to the "sing zone."

And when they got there?

He sang.

No, he didn't sing—he rocked.

DeMarcus belted out the first line of the song with so much power, my hands slipped off the guitar. They'd gone totally numb because all the blood had just rushed to my eyeballs as they tried to explode out of my head. He was incredible. A few strangers crowded around us. Some of them even joined in on the chorus.

I'd never heard anyone who could keep up with Freddie Mercury. Everyone around us was stomp-stomp-clapping away when suddenly the music stopped and the screen flashed red. I was sure the machine must've melted, but it turned out that I'd totally forgotten to start playing.

"Oh—I'm sorry! I didn't even think—"

"That's okay," he said, smiling. "It was still fun."

The small crowd cleared out and I looked back at Sarah, expecting her to be watching DeMarcus with gigantic cartoony hearts in her eyes. She wasn't, though. She had her fists propped up on her hips, scowling. Troy and Bobby were laughing, pointing our way.

DeMarcus took a deep breath, looking more energized than I'd ever seen. "You want some advice, Dillon?"

I nodded.

"As soon as you can, find out who you are and go for it. Forget what everyone else thinks, because if you don't—" He glanced at Sarah. Then his eyes fell and he put the mike back on the little stand. "If you don't, you're gonna get stuck being someone you're not."

DeMarcus gave me a slap on the shoulder and grabbed his jacket. He took a few steps and glanced over his shoulder.

"And trust me, man. Nothing feels worse than that."

24

▲▲▲▲▲▲▲▲▲

Mom's voice crashed through my door. "Sweetie! We have to leave in an hour and I'm not taking you if you don't at least brush your teeth!"

As if on cue, the sour taste of morning breath hit my tongue. Gross. I slid my legs over the side of my bed, groaning the whole way. I should've been about to pop with excitement. It was the Big Saturday. The day of the Heartland Dance Challenge. But my brain was still crashing into itself trying to piece together the *what I wants* with the *what I needs*.

I scooted the toothbrush around on my teeth for a few seconds, just long enough to paint my mouth with a layer of mint, and hopped in the shower. When I finally got to the kitchen, my parents were standing next to the table. Mom was wearing a smile way too big for how crummy I felt.

"What?" I said, stopping at the edge of the linoleum.

Silence. Mom elbowed Dad in the side. He shot her a quick *Was that necessary?* look and she replied with her own *You're two seconds away from getting elbowed again* glare.

He took a deep breath. "I think I owe you an apology." I started to ask what he was talking about, but Dad kept going. "When you started taking karate, I didn't waste any time making sure you had whatever you needed. When you told me you were trying out for football, I bet I went by every sports store in the county to look at equipment."

Dad laughed like he was deep in a memory of a relative he'd lost years ago. Probably thinking of when his son wasn't a friend-dumped, scholarship-chasing dance traitor.

"Your mom and I did a lot of talking. Well, she did most of the talking. Or all of it, really—"

Another elbow.

"—but she made a good point. Our company helps new businesses get their feet off the ground. To find what they need to get started and then support them when they take off. And I haven't been doing that with you. Or more specifically with your dancing. And I should be." Dad reached behind him and grabbed something off the counter. "So consider this a small invest-ment in your future."

Mom pulled a chair out and led me to it. Dad handed her a small box and she placed it in my hands. A present. It should have thrilled me. Especially since it had something to do with dance. But I'd been slowly deflating inside since August.

I peeled off the lid and let it fall to the floor. I pushed the layer of tissue paper to the side and my breath caught in my throat.

No way. My fingers brushed against the smooth fabric. I pinched the corners of the black material and stood. My mouth fell open and a long exhale escaped with a "Whoa."

I couldn't believe what I was holding.

Tights.

Not panty hose. Not football pants . . .

Real dance tights.

"The website said those should fit a twelve-year-old," Mom said. "But if they don't, we can exchange them. Or if you don't like the style or—"

"They're perfect."

Mom let out a sigh of relief. "Okay, good. I overheard you talking about dance tights a couple of times. We *were* going to get you the shoes, too, but there were so many different kinds."

"No, this is enough," I said. "Really." I should've been

running to my bedroom to try them on. And I would've if I felt like I deserved them. My legs sort of gave out and I fell into my chair.

Mom put her hand against my forehead. "Are you feeling okay? You look pale, sweetie."

"I'm fine. Just nervous, I guess."

"Don't be. You made it this far. I could tell those judges loved you."

"You didn't see their faces, Mom. They thought I was a joke."

"We saw their faces just fine!"

I rolled the waistband of the tights between my thumb and finger. "Yeah, well, did you hear them when I talked about my audition video?" I couldn't remember if the judges had actually groaned or if it was just my imagination. But in my head they had practically torn their eyes out when I'd answered their questions about it.

Dad leaned against the counter beside Mom. "Well, maybe if you'd cut the part with your underwear or—"

Mom's eyes snapped wide.

Dad sighed. "I thought your video was great."

"Whatever. You've never liked me dancing."

"No, that's not true."

"Um, are you forgetting the whole *dancing is risky* thing you said at dinner?"

I've never seen my dad nervous. But when Mom dug

her knuckles into her hips, he looked like he was two seconds away from breaking out into the biggest freak-out sweat I'd ever witnessed.

Dad shook his head like he was about to come up with an excuse. But then he took a step toward the table, putting the chair in between him and Mom. "Okay, yes. I do remember that. And the truth is it *still* makes me a little uneasy knowing you may be dancing through high school and get picked on."

"See! You don't get it, so you think it's stupid!"

"You're right, I don't get it. But I've never thought it was stupid. And so what if I don't totally understand it." He sat down beside me.

I looked at him. There was a layer of guilt on his face. Something I'd never seen when he was talking to me about dancing.

"My point is you should do what makes you happy. Even if I don't understand it. Some of our clients have pretty crazy business ideas, and not everyone gets those."

Mom mouthed, *Alan Scapelli.*

"But that doesn't stop me from taking a chance on them. And—" Dad put a hand on my shoulder. "It shouldn't stop you, either."

He hugged me. It was the first time he'd ever talked to me about dance without laughing or shaking his head. When he leaned back, his eyes were teary. He played it off, saying, "Boy, football's made you strong, kiddo.

Nearly crushed my windpipe." He stood and Mom nearly tackled him with a hug of her own.

Dad was right. I needed to dance. The moves Sarah had been teaching me may not have fit like they were supposed to. But maybe that's what being a real dancer was all about. Dancing the way you *need* to instead of just the way you *want* to.

I looked down at my tights.

I'd made it this far training with Sarah without my brain exploding.

Surely I could dance her routine one more time.

Mom asked if I wanted some eggs, but my stomach had drawn up to the size of a pea. The idea of anything but bland cereal made it scream in agony. I kept my tights right beside me on the table. Close enough to be near, but not so close that my milk would get on them.

When I went downstairs to change, my phone was buzzing. I ran over, grabbing it off my bed, my heart hammering out a quick-step beat. Maybe it was Kassie. Who else would call this early?

But it wasn't.

It was an event reminder. *Saturday, November 9: dance competition.*

I stuffed the phone in my duffel bag along with everything else I needed for today. I wasn't sure why, but I even took the Dizzee Freekz pin off my backpack and attached it to the side pocket. As I threw myself into the car for the drive to Davis County High School, the worry, the freaking out, the feeling that nobody got me and my ninja freestyle, faded away. It was time to man up.

It was time to finish this thing. Time to step up and do what it was going to take to finally become a real dancer.

And there was only one way to do that.

I had to strut onto that stage wearing a pair of tights and dance like I'd never danced before.

▲▲▲▲▲▲▲▲▲

It reminded me of a zombie movie.

The parking lot was completely filled. People had pulled onto the grass, stopping their SUVs and expensive cars all catty-cornered. The ones who had already gotten out of their vehicles were flooding into the high school like it was the one place the undead couldn't break into.

When we got inside, the hallway was packed with dancers of all ages and sizes. Parents with matching shirts, some with jackets with studio names on them. And everyone talking, laughing, taking up every bit of noise-space and not leaving any for me to even hear myself think.

"Darn it!" Dad said, making me jump. "We should've

made a poster." He nodded at a group of adults, each one with a homemade sign completely decorated with glitter and blown-up pictures of a dancer's face.

My parents were pros at humiliating me at my football games with nothing but a wave and a phone. Giving them a poster would've been a guaranteed disaster.

I looked around for Kassie and Carson even though I knew they wouldn't be there. Plus the place was wall-to-wall spandex and duffel bags. No way I was gonna see any more than a few feet around me. Luckily, there were signs posted telling us where to go.

The crowd inched forward toward one of four desks, each handling one section of the alphabet, signing up competitors and handing out half sheets of paper with big numbers printed on them. I poked my head through the crowd, searching for the *P–S* table, but I was blocked by a wall of neon orange tracksuits.

"Chuck, don't be afraid to get a little pushy. Everyone else is doing it," Mom said with her hand on Dad's back, urging him forward.

"I'm not going to barrel through the crowd, Carol. I could step on a kid or something."

I couldn't see my mom's face, but I could feel her eyes roll. She took a deep breath and nudged me to the left, weaving me through a group of dancers.

"Hi there. Last name?" the girl at the table asked. She was pretty. Her eyes were the same color as Kassie's.

Except Kassie's were a little more hazelly. And Kassie also had longer eyelashes. And better eyebrows—

Stop it! I forced my thoughts back in the right direction. I couldn't get distracted. Not now. It was time to focus.

"P-Parker?" My voice was shaking. Like I was in the middle of a snowstorm without a jacket.

She thumbed through a small tub of folders and pulled one out. "Here we go. Dillon Parker?"

I nodded. Mom grabbed my shoulder, making me jump. "Ooh, this is so exciting!" she said.

The almost-as-pretty-as-Kassie girl glanced inside the folder and handed it to me. "Okay, Dillon, here you go. Just follow the signs back to the dressing rooms. You'll see one marked for Dance-Splosion."

Mom immediately dove into the information inside the folder. "Sweetie, look! You have your own number!" She held up a sticker about the size of a phone.

019.

My stomach quaked. Surely that didn't mean I was the nineteenth one to dance. "Is there a schedule in there?"

Mom looked through the papers. "Right here."

I tore it out of her hands and read it. Nothing about the scholarship, but solos were up first. I planted my hands on my knees and tried to breathe like I wasn't about to pass out.

"Dillon, what's wrong?" Mom asked, rubbing my back.

"Uh, just nervous."

"You're ready for this. I know you are."

I stood back up. My head went a little woozy, but that only lasted for a second.

"Good luck, kiddo," Dad said. "We're going to go find a good seat."

Mom stuffed my tag into my shirt. "If you need anything, just text us. You have your phone?"

I held my duffel bag up. My hands were shaking. Not just trembling. I'm talking earthquake in my arms. If I had been holding a can of soda right then, the entire thing would've turned to fizz and spewed out the top.

"Don't be nervous. You're going to do great." Dad patted me on the back and Mom followed it up with a hug. I told them thanks, keeping it short so I wouldn't have to hear how bad my voice was trembling.

I opened the door to the dressing room. It was actually a small classroom with a tall black screen at the back, probably where we could get changed. Standing near the door was a guy wearing a yellow shirt that had VOLUNTEER printed on it.

Several dancers were grouped together, scattered around the room. Most were just talking. A few were walking through their routines. I looked around for Sarah, but didn't see her.

Kenton and Avery were tucked in the back. I walked over to join them, keeping my mouth shut and my game face on. I sat in the floor across the room from Avery and began stretching my hamstrings. Since I'd been practicing with Sarah I'd become pretty limber. Not split-worthy or anything, but at least now I could touch my nose to my knees without feeling like the backs of my legs were going to rip in half.

I unzipped my bag and pulled out my new tights, folding them into a small square beside me. I wanted them to see what I'd brought. That I meant business.

"No football pants?" Kenton said with a smirk.

I shook my head. "Not today." No smile. I wasn't about to tell him I still had my football tights in my duffel bag.

"They look brand-new," Avery said.

I kicked the compliment away, meeting her smile with a quick nod. I hated to do that, but I couldn't let the other two get in my head. This was war. Plus it was hard for me to look at her, remembering what had happened last time she danced.

Kenton's eyes landed on Avery and her leggings. He looked like he was about to say something, but he didn't. Instead, he just laughed. She had on the same ones that had made her fall during the audition. I couldn't be sure, but I thought I saw a few safety pins holding one of them together. She saw me staring and quickly pulled her foot toward her.

I forced my eyes ahead. Away from Kenton. Away from Avery and her torn legging. I was there to win. Even if it meant stepping on a few pointed toes.

I ran through the routine Sarah had taught me. The

kickless, punchless routine. I couldn't stand it. Not because I hadn't come up with the moves, but because the steps weren't made for me. They were like a pair of football cleats ten sizes too big. And I had to wear them on the most important game of my life.

On the third mental run-through, a muffled roar poured into the room. Cheers. Applause. Screams.

The competition had started.

26

▲▲▲▲▲▲▲▲▲

I stood at the edge of the stage behind a huge black curtain with a few other dancers.

Almost every seat in the auditorium was filled. The announcer flipped the card in his hand over and spoke. "All right, everyone, are you ready to have your worlds rocked?"

He jogged around onstage, holding the mike out to the crowd as they went nuts. A huge purple HEART-LAND DANCE CHALLENGE banner ruffled behind him. The sparkles that filled the letters ART inside the word HEARTLAND sent off waves of little reflections dancing across the floor. When the audience finally calmed down, he continued.

"We at the HDC like to keep things pretty small here,

but this year—" The guy stopped in the middle of the stage, looking out toward the crowd. "This year we've got the biggest turnout we've ever had, folks!"

The crowd cheered as he pumped his fists into the air, running around the stage like he'd eaten an entire bag of sugar for breakfast.

"We'll be starting off tonight's competition with the solos in the Mini Division and working our way up from there." The guy went on. Across the stage, there was another volunteer standing with a small group of kids. I guessed those were the Mini Division dancers. They couldn't have been much older than kindergartners.

The crowd roared, snapping me out of whatever daze I was in. When I craned my neck to look over the dancers in front of me, the announcer was leaving the stage as a tiny girl in a sparkly orange outfit strutted on. I watched the first few routines. Even the Minis were good. Especially number 011.

The little guy had done a hip-hop routine that actually made me jealous.

Of a preschooler.

I pulled myself away from the curtain. My stomach was break-dancing in my gut and I wasn't sure how much longer I'd be able to keep my measly bowl of cereal down. When I spun around, I almost ran right into Kenton.

"You're not nervous, are you?" he said with a smirk

that I wanted to peel right off his face. I glanced down at his number: 018. I couldn't decide whether going before him or after him would've been better. So instead, I tried not to think about it and headed away from the wing.

Avery was standing by herself, bouncing up and down on her toes. "Hey, Dillon," she said, waving. She sounded about as freaked out as I felt. For some reason that made me feel a little better. "A lot more people here than I thought."

"Yeah," I said.

The crowd's cheers echoed backstage. A volunteer trotted up, glancing at the sticker on my chest. Then at Avery's—013. "Avery Yates? You're up next. Just head to the wing and wait for them to call you."

Avery gave me one last shaky-handed wave. She stopped beside Kenton, keeping her head down. Probably so she wouldn't accidentally look at the jerky grin that I was sure his face was still drowning in.

I glanced down at her legging, already starting to droop. *Don't do it, Dillon. You're here to win.* Brain was pulling my eyes away, but heart was already sending me forward. I had to win, but not because her legging sent her flying off the stage.

"Hey, hold on." I pulled the string out of my sweat pants' waistband and knelt down beside her leg. "Before you go out."

"What are you—" she said, but then stopped as I pulled her legging up and tied it over her calf with the string.

"Just in case. Good luck."

She stared at her leg for a second and then looked up at me, pulling me into a hug. My breath caught in my chest. Giving her a string didn't make up for what I'd done. But I couldn't have let her dance like that. She smiled and walked onstage. Beside me, Kenton rolled his eyes.

"Shut up," I mumbled.

I hiked my sweats up and focused on the audience, trying to find my parents. Instead, my eyes landed on Kassie, Carson, and Austin sitting about halfway up on the end of an aisle.

I grabbed the edge of the curtain. What were they doing there? My first reaction was to run back down the side hallway into the auditorium. Dive into their arms and tell them all how much I'd missed them.

But then, a second reaction took over.

Fear.

Because I realized they probably weren't there for me. They had to be there for Sarah. What if Kassie had changed her mind again and was planning on jumping up on the stage and crashing through the award ceremony like a human wrecking ball?

Avery's music began and the lights dimmed.

I ran back to the dressing room and grabbed my phone. I couldn't text Kassie. She probably wouldn't answer me. Austin wouldn't, either.

To: Carson

Message: is kassie going thru with her plan???

I waited. Inhale. Exhale. I was sucking down tiny gulps of air twice as fast as I should. The dressing room started spinning. Everything was going blurry.

I started shaking. No, I was being shaken. Sarah had me by the shoulders, trying to bring me back to life.

"Don't do this, Dillon! I swear, if you faint before they announce your win, I'll kill you!"

"I—need—siddown," I mumbled.

Sarah pulled me around the corner into a classroom and sat me down in a chair. I rubbed my arm, still feeling the pinch where her fingers had been.

"What is wrong with you?" she snapped.

"They're here!"

"*Who's* here?"

"Carson and Austin and—and Kassie. In the audience."

"So?"

There was no tiptoeing around it anymore. "Kassie's here to—" I drew in a long breath, imagining the air soaking into my lungs was the courage I needed. "She's, um, she's going to—"

My phone vibrated in my hand. I glanced down at the screen.

Carson: no. she decided not to, remember?

Sarah waved her hands in front of me. "Would you just spit it out?"

I would've, except I didn't know what to spit out. If Kassie wasn't there to finish her plan, then why'd she show up?

"Whatever," Sarah said, grabbing my wrist. "Let's go."

I pulled away. "Just give me a minute, okay? This doesn't make any sense."

"What doesn't make sense is you getting all weird right before your solo." She made another grab for my hand, but I dodged her grip.

"Geez, calm down! Why do you even care if I dance, anyway?"

"It doesn't matter," she said, waving me forward. "Now come on."

"Yeah, but you already know Kassie's not competing."

Sarah's face went rigid. "I know that, Dillon."

"But it doesn't make—"

"I have to show my dad I can do this, okay? He thinks me teaching is the stupidest idea ever. But it's what I want to do. It's what I've always wanted to do."

The image of her drawing popped in my head. *Arts*

eMotion. Her made-up studio. Maybe she was telling the truth. I studied her face for a few seconds. "If all you want to do is teach, then why'd you steal Kassie's solo?"

"I already told you, I didn't. And you can stop looking at me like I'm a liar, because I'm telling the truth." Sarah's jaw clenched and for a second I thought she was just going to say something mean. "I told Kassie she should go for it. I even offered to help her with the choreography. But he wouldn't let me."

I started to ask who the *he* was, but I already knew the answer. "Your dad."

Sarah stared down at her feet. "When he found out what happened, he told me he'd rather pull me out of Dance-Splosion than see me give up a solo to another dancer. But—he did what he had to do."

She stood like that for a few seconds before she looked back up at me, her face all stony and blank. She was doing her best to pretend she was okay, but I knew she wasn't. Because what she'd just said—all of the junk she'd ever told me about the rules, the pain, ignoring friends—wasn't really from her. It was from her dad. And I knew how she felt because I'd done the same thing before. Everyone has. We'll hear something so many times that we start to believe it. Like eating too much chocolate gives you zits. But no matter how much we think it belongs in our head, it still sounds wrong coming out of our mouths. Because the words aren't right. They don't fit.

"This is why you have to get ready," Sarah said. "I can't let him see me mess this up. Because if you don't get out there and nail your solo today, he'll be right. Just like he always is. And I can't let that happen, Dillon."

"Wait, so—you're just using me. To prove something to your dad?"

"Seriously? Now is *not* the time to get all dramatic."

"I'm not being dramatic! I actually thought you may have been helping me because you wanted me to win."

"I do! I mean, yeah, I want to show my dad I have what it takes to be a good teacher, but—" She took a step forward. "I still want you to win. For you, too."

Whatever. I'd been used. Twice. By Kassie *and* Sarah.

I was Dillon Parker, the plunger. The tool everyone needed to do their dirty work for them.

Except Kassie had never actually sent me headfirst into the toilet. In fact, she'd tried to pull me out, but in a way I wouldn't let her.

"Listen, we don't have time to talk about this," Sarah said, walking toward the door. "You're on in just a few minutes." She stormed out into the hallway, but my feet were cemented to the floor. Something wasn't right. My brain was shuffling around all the chunks of the last four months and nothing was making sense. Like a group dance with only half of it choreographed.

"What're you doing?" Sarah was holding on to the doorway, her hand stuck out like she was trying to rescue me from sinking.

"I don't know," I said. My feet kicked into gear, but they didn't take me to the door. They took me back and forth from one side of the room to the other.

Before I knew it, Sarah was right beside me with her hands back on my shoulders. "Look, all you have to do it get out there and dance."

"That's the thing, Sarah! I don't even know if I want to." I shrugged her hands away. "This whole thing has been so weird and now my crew's out there. Besides, I've seen who I'm up against. Those other two are way better than me."

Sarah balled up her hands in front of her. "None of that even matters. Just get out there and keep your promise. It's the least you could do, since I got you a scholarship. Now *come on!*"

"What do you mean you *got* me a scholarship?"

Sarah cocked an eyebrow at me. "Do you really think you made it this far just by your dancing?"

"But—I'm getting better. You've even said so yourself."

"True. But better isn't great. You should be thanking me."

I fell down onto the chair next to my duffel bag.

"Would it help if I said I already know you're going to win?"

Every bit of the air left my chest at once. I had to force myself to suck in a breath. I tried to say *What are you talking about?* but all that came out was, "Whaaa?"

"Trust me, it wasn't easy. But all you have to do is get out there and dance and that scholarship is yours. Isn't that what you wanted?"

A shiver raced from the top of my head down to my toes.

One more dance.

Three weeks full of dance classes.

A lifetime of dancing. *Real* dancing.

My heart pounded in my chest. In my fingertips. In my ears. And it was screaming for me to get off my butt and do it.

So why wasn't I on my feet? Why wasn't I running out the door, ready to hop onstage and snatch a guaranteed summer scholarship from the air?

The music from the stage faded out, leaving the *ba-bum, ba-bum* of my heartbeat crashing in my head. Sarah was tapping her wrist, trying to tell me we didn't have time. But I couldn't hear her voice.

All I heard was *ba-bum, ba-bum, ba-bum . . .*

Get-off . . .

Your-butt . . .

And-dance . . .

Something bright caught the corner of my eye. I looked down at my duffel bag. My Dizzee Freekz pin.

And that's when it happened.

CLICK!

Something in my head slid into place. And it didn't just click inside. It clicked everywhere. It clicked so hard I felt it vibrate through my entire body. That little piece of the puzzle that'd been colliding with every part of my brain had finally found a spot to rest.

My heart was telling me to dance. But not for myself. Not for that scholarship.

I turned to Sarah. "I'm sorry."

Her smile disappeared. "Sorry about what?"

"I can't do it. I have to drop out."

The color drained from her face, making the makeup around her eyes and cheeks look even brighter. "You can't do this to me, Dillon."

But I was already zipping my bag back up and heading toward the door.

"If—if you do this, you'll never get into Dance-Splosion!" Sarah's hands were balled into fists. *"Never!"*

I looked down at the pin. The Dizzee Freekz. My crew. My best friends. The ones who let me just be me. The ones I'd turned my back on.

"I'm . . . okay with that."

FWOOSH!

The air rushed into my lungs as the vise grip that had been around my chest disappeared. I slid by Sarah, pausing just long enough to say "I'm sorry," and then barreled down the hallway, away from the stage, toward the main entrance. I pulled my phone out.

To: Kassie, Carson, Austin
Message: Get 2 hallway. We have 2 talk!!!!

27

▲▲▲▲▲▲▲▲▲

Number 017 was up.

I stuck my ear to the door, listening to the music when—

WHACK!

The door opened right on my nose and a flood of tears poured into my eyes.

"Oh—I'm so sorry!" Kassie said, reaching for my face.

I waved, letting her know I was fine. Carson and Austin piled in beside her.

"You sure?" she asked, and pulled her arms back. "Okay, so—what's up?" The concern was gone from her voice. No surprise there.

"Yeah, you never use that many exclamation points," Carson added.

I flexed my face, stretching my nose. "Why are you all here?"

Before she could answer, Sarah came stomping around the corner, hitting the brakes when she saw us. Austin took a step behind Carson.

Kassie scowled. "What's going on?"

Sarah ignored her and lasered in on me. "Dillon, don't be stupid, just come back and—"

"Hey, don't talk to him like that!" Carson said.

"Back off. This isn't any of your business."

Carson tanked the oxygen levels in the room after he sucked in all the air with one quick mega-gasp. Or maybe my head was spinning because I'd only eaten half my cereal that morning. More than likely, though, it was because I was scared I'd just brought two of Sunnydale's biggest enemies together in one room.

"No, it *is* my business," Carson said. "Dillon's still my friend."

"He's my friend, too!" Sarah's eyes jumped to me like she almost expected me to laugh and say *Whatever!* But I didn't. And not just because Carson beat me to it.

"Whatever! I know exactly what you're doing." Carson took a step forward, speaking louder every time Sarah opened her mouth. "You're just playing one of your little games, waiting for the right time to bring everything crashing down on top of him so you can get exactly what you want and make yourself feel better. Just like you did with Kassie. Just like you did with *me*!"

Carson's eyes were about to spill over with tears. He may have been the skinniest guy I'd ever known, but he was also the toughest. I'd never seen him get upset like that.

"I did what I did because I had to protect—" Sarah shook her head. "I never meant to hurt you, Carson. Or you, Kassie, I swear. I never even wanted that solo. I wanted *you* to dance, because you were amazing."

Kassie crossed her arms. "Then why'd you audition for it behind my back?"

Sarah walked over to a bench and fell into it. When she finally unburied her head from her hands, she looked pale. Almost sick. "I didn't want to. I told my dad you deserved a shot at that national title just as much as I did. But he told me if I was going to start handing over all of my solos, he'd make me quit Dance-Splosion."

Kassie's face was the picture of shock. Carson and Austin stared at her like they were halfway expecting her to rip into Sarah at any second. But all she did was keep her eyes glued to the floor. She shoved her hands in her back pockets.

Sarah started to speak, then stopped. Her fingers played at the end of her ponytail. "I'm sorry. I should've said no."

Kassie looked back up. Her mouth was scrunched up

like it was trying to smile through a wall of hurt. "Probably good we didn't go through with our plan then, huh?"

"Plan?"

"We were going to have Dillon sabotage the contest," Carson said, still looking mad. "I'm not totally convinced we still shouldn't do it."

"I never wanted to," Austin said, his voice sounding hoarse, like he'd almost forgotten how to speak. Sarah swiveled her head toward him. He added a weak "Hi," and almost stuck his finger up his nose trying to adjust his glasses.

"Guess I can't blame you," Sarah said. "I was pretty awful."

Kassie shook her head. "No. You weren't. But I'm sort of feeling like a terrible person right now." She turned to me. I thought she'd be angry at me for putting her in a situation where she had to apologize to Sarah. I expected her eyes to be so cold they could've frozen a volcano. What I saw, though, was something different. "I never should've put you in the middle of this," she said softly. "I'm sorry."

"Seriously? I'm the one who should be apologizing, Kass. I wanted to get better at dancing. I was tired of always letting you down. All I did was end up acting like a butt and making my friends hate me."

Austin snorted out a laugh.

"We don't hate you, Dillon. And as much as I like you getting all sensitive, it's going to have to wait." She tapped the sticker on the front of my shirt. "You need to get going. You're up soon."

"I can't. I was wrong. This whole thing was wrong."

"No, it's not, Dill. You made it this far. You can't just give up." Kassie nodded to Carson and Austin. "That's why we're here. We should've been supporting you."

"You're joking."

"I know you think you've been holding us back. But I'm the one who's been doing that. If you wanted to learn different moves, I should've taught you. And— and I didn't."

"You'll always be part of the Dizzee Freekz," Carson said. Even Austin nodded.

Sarah stood up, begging me with her eyes. I couldn't believe what I was about to do. My opportunity was staring at me in the face and I was going to turn my back on it.

I walked over to her. "You don't need me to dance that solo.

She bit the edge of her lip. "Please don't. If you drop out, my dad—"

"He'll be mad. Disappointed. You'll never hear the end of it. Trust me, I know how parents can be. But Avery deserves to win that scholarship. And I can't go out there and steal it away from her. I can't do what your dad did to Kassie."

Sarah took a deep breath, her chest hitching halfway through.

"You're an incredible dancer. And a really good teacher, too," I said. "No matter what I decide."

"But what if he makes me quit? He already threatened to do that once."

"If he does, then he's an idiot. No offense."

She wiped her eyes, laughing underneath the tears. "I wish you'd tell that to him."

"Tell him yourself," Kassie said. "Get out there and do it with your dance."

I smiled at Kassie. She smiled right back.

"I can't do that. Not with what we've already choreographed."

"Yes, you can," I said. "Just forget all the rules for once. Forget the steps and the moves and just tell an awesome story. If your dad's out there, he'll hear it. Trust me."

Sarah drew in a long breath. There was still fear hiding in her eyes, but not as much. "Okay." She glanced over my shoulder at Kassie, Carson, and Austin. "Thank you."

Kassie dug something out of her pocket and tossed it to Sarah. A Dizzee Freekz pin. "For good luck," Kassie said.

Sarah stared down at it. She shot Kassie a quick *thank you* smile and turned toward the hallway.

"Hey, before you go," I said, putting myself in between

her and my friends. "Can you do one thing for me? It's gonna sound weird, but can you look at Austin and tell him hi?"

A flash of confusion flooded into her eyes. But then it disappeared like she realized why I'd asked her. Sarah stepped around me and said, "Hi, Austin." She even added in a little finger-wiggle wave.

Austin stood there, slack-jawed and eyes bulging, as Sarah walked off.

He'd finally got his *hi* from her.

A volunteer poked his head through the doors. "You Dillon Parker?" he asked, looking at the 019 on my shirt.

Applause rang through the theater. Kenton must've finished.

Everyone's head swung toward me. I looked at the volunteer. "Sorry. Dillon's gone." I tore off my sticker. "I'm the Kung Fu Kid."

Carson exploded into a clapping fit, nearly making me jump out of my own shoes.

The guy at the door rolled his eyes. "Well, when Dillon comes back, can you tell him he needs to get to the wings in the next thirty seconds?"

The judge in the auditorium called my name. "Last chance," Kassie said.

"I'm not a solo kind of guy. I belong with you all. With my crew. If you'll take me back."

Kassie's cheeks went a little red. She pushed the stray

curl behind her ear. I missed seeing her do that. "Us freaks have to stick together, don't we?"

"Welcome back, dude," Austin said. "And no hard feelings for turning into a butt."

A loud sigh popped out of the volunteer. "Okay, so—"

"Oh my gosh, get a clue and stop ruining our moment," Carson said.

The volunteer mumbled something into his headset and went back inside.

"So did, um, Patrick come with you guys?" I asked.

All three of them erupted into a loud groan.

"Bro," Carson said in a goofy voice. "How about you jump this way, bro. *Bro, bro, bro*—I'm so glad we got rid of him."

Austin dragged his hand down his face. "Can you believe he rewrote my zombie script? Said it wasn't the direction he wanted to see it go in."

"Yeah, it wasn't really working out with Patrick," Kassie added.

"So what now?" Austin asked. "Want to check out some of the routines?"

"What? No, we can still make it—we preregistered."

"No! Dillon, I can't," Kassie said.

I put my hands on her shoulders. "Yes, you can. And you won't have to do it alone. You'll be with us." I wanted to say more. Something inspirational like all the coaches in the movies say to their football players. But my brain was stuck on staring at her eyes.

She must've known what I was going for, though, because she said, "We're not ready, though. We didn't bring our clothes."

"We'll dance in what we're wearing. But not you, Carson. You don't wanna dance in skinny jeans, trust me." I grabbed the waistband of my sweats and yanked them down to my shoes. I stood back up, smiling.

"Whoa," Kassie said, pinching the fabric on my leg. "These are real."

"My football pants are still in my bag. I can wear those. Carson can wear these."

"Ew, no," Carson said, scrunching his face up in disgust. "All your butt sweat—"

"I just put them on like twenty minutes ago. My butt doesn't sweat that much."

Carson shrugged, still looking a little grossed out. He unbuttoned his shirt, exposing the rainbow-glittered work of art his mom had made.

"I might have another T-shirt in my bag, too." My phone buzzed inside my duffel bag. I checked the message. It was Mom asking if something was wrong and why I didn't dance. I sent her a quick reply to let her know there was a change in the lineup.

Carson scrunched his mouth up like he was thinking about it. "You know, this is probably the ugliest shirt

I've ever seen. The only reason I wore it was so my parents would quit bugging me to. Plus I knew nobody would see it."

He pulled the bottom of his shirt out, looking at the words.

carson "c-note" evans

"My mom and dad are completely insane. But I guess I like them like that. The shirt stays. Now hand over your butt-sweaty tights before I change my mind."

"So you're actually doing this?" Austin asked.

"*We're* doing this," I said. "Including our director. Especially since he's got a music video to finish."

A smile stretched across Austin's face. He clapped his hands together like I'd just handed him a brand-new camera signed by Steven Spielberg. "That's what I'm talking about!"

We all looked at Kassie. She tugged at the string hanging from her hood. Our routine's fate was dancing on a paper-thin layer of ice. With one word, she could send it crashing through, sinking.

But then she smiled.

And the entire hallway lit up.

"All right. Let's do it," she said. "I'll pull the song up on the way."

I took off with everyone following behind me. As

soon as I rounded the corner where the registration tables were, I found the *A–D* table and yelled out, "We're here! Dizzee Freekz with a *Z*!"

We ran up to it, panting. The girl behind the table smiled and flipped through the plastic tub holding the last few folders. "Cutting it a little close, aren't you?"

"We still have time, don't we?"

"Just barely." She picked up a folder and handed it to me. "That's a cute name. Dizzee Freekz."

"Thanks," I said, trying not to sound offended. We weren't cute. We were fierce.

"Dressing rooms are down the hall. Make sure you wear your numbers at all times."

"Okay, cool." I opened the folder. Number 083.

"We already have your music?"

Kassie handed her phone over to the girl. "Can we use this? It's the only thing that has our music. All you have to do is hit play."

The girl took the phone just as DeMarcus came jogging around the corner from the holding room.

Carson's hands shot to his hair, pushing back his bangs. If he turned any redder, someone would've mistaken him for a gigantic cherry Pixie Stick.

"Hey, guys. Sarah told me to bring you these." He held out a handful of safety pins. "She said the numbers stick on, but they peel off super easy."

"Aww!" Carson said, taking a couple.

"So, you guys are really competing?" DeMarcus asked.

We all glanced at each other, smiling. Darn right we were competing.

The Dizzee Freekz were back.

28

▲▲▲▲▲▲▲▲▲

The solo routines flew by.

Number 023 was the first duet. It was a tap routine. I'd seen better, but not from a pair of elementary-age boys. Each dance seemed to put the one before it to shame.

A guy in a volunteer shirt pointed at Austin and De-Marcus. "You two need a number."

"We're not dancers," Austin replied. "We're, uh, managers. I'm the lead manager. He's, like, my assistant."

Apparently the guy didn't care, because he just shrugged and jotted something down on his clipboard. DeMarcus held out his fist. Austin hesitated for a second, then bumped his against it.

"We're gonna have to be amazing," I said.

"Then we will be," Kassie said.

"I know, it's just—we need something to give us that edge. Something like—"

Behind me, Carson gasped. When we spun around, he smiled, his face turning a pale pink. "Sorry," he said, grabbing his jeans out of my duffel bag. "I know what we could do. I found this a while ago when we were still looking. It's the lift."

He pulled out his phone and held it out like it was made of paper-thin glass. We gathered around as he pulled up a video and hit play. I didn't know who the dancers were. Probably pros. Toes, back, neck, lines— all perfect. But the part that caught everyone's attention was when the guy turned his back to the girl. She ran up to him—I'm talking about a full-on sprint—and jumped. As soon as her feet left the ground, he spun around and caught her in this sort of hug-type catch.

We all mumbled "Whoa" at the same time. It was that good.

"It's the one," Carson said, pausing the video. "It has to be, guys."

"Yeah, but . . ." I said, my face feeling a little hotter than normal as I thought about Kassie jumping into my arms like that. "It's not really a lift, is it?"

"It's better than a lift. And I bet you no other crew will have something like this."

Austin scrolled back the video and hit play again. "I don't know, man. This is a serious move."

"Exactly. It's gorgeous."

"Austin's right. I don't know if I can catch her like that."

"I've seen you at practice, man," DeMarcus said, slapping me on the shoulder. "If you can catch a ball I throw, you can catch anything."

Kassie and I looked at each other—me feeling like my face was about to catch fire and her chewing her lip.

"Yeah, but—"

"I trust you," Kassie said. "We should go for it." She took a tiny step toward me. I stared into her hazel eyes and forgot about everything else. There was just the dance. There was just us.

She trusted me.

I drew in a long breath. "I'm in."

Carson stuffed his phone back into the duffel bag. "This is going to be so cool!"

After the duets were finished, the group numbers were up. 057—a group ballet performance with music that nearly sang me to sleep. 061—a killer contemporary with a funky alien theme. And 080—a Broadway routine with cowboys and cowgirls dancing around a poker table. Seeing it made me think of Avery.

Then, before I knew it, we were being herded toward the curtain by the backstage guy.

It was the coldest spot on earth. The icy glares that were being thrown around near the curtains had turned the place into a freezer.

Two more routines to go. Besides the one time Carson adjusted his tights, grumbling something about "butt sweat," no one said anything. We just stood in the wing, looking out onto the stage.

I went to my tiptoes, freezing when I spotted our next competitors—Sarah and her Barbies.

They were sitting onstage, each girl bent over one leg stretched out in front of her. As the music started, they floated up to a standing position, windmilling their arms over their heads and into a backbend that made it look like they were about to snap in half.

Sarah was the first one to come out of it. She straightened into a move I remember her making me do over and over—a retiré—and broke into a series of spins. Her team followed. At first. But then Sarah leaped into the air and the Barbies stumbled back like they were scared of her.

For the next minute and a half, it was all Sarah.

Moving. Reaching. Turning. Her Barbies were doing everything possible to keep up. Probably. I didn't know because I couldn't stop watching Sarah.

She was finally letting herself just dance.

Kassie looked over her shoulder. There was no anger on her face. No jealousy in her eyes. "She's really doing it," she whispered.

Sarah was putting it all out there, outdancing her teammates as she poured her heart out on the stage.

The music rolled its way toward the end, fading with the last note as Sarah came to a rest in front of the other two.

We all clapped. Carson was applauding harder than all of us. I turned toward Austin. He mouthed *Wow*, and beside him, DeMarcus gave me a wide-eyed nod.

The crowd finally died down and Sarah and her crew exited right toward us. The Barbies pranced by first, looking past us like we weren't even there. But Sarah smiled, turning her head so we could see her hair. Right at the top of her blond ponytail was our pin.

As soon as they cleared the side curtain, Sarah's friends spun around, clawing their way toward Sarah, asking her things like "What were you doing out there?" "Why'd you mess everything up?" "What's wrong with you?"

Sarah's response?

She just smiled and let them hiss. After a few seconds, a volunteer came over and hushed them quiet.

"That was amazing, Sarah," Kassie said. "The dance, I mean."

Sarah never got a word out, because Black-Haired Barbie stepped forward with a smirk that had *nasty* written all over it. "Too bad you all won't get a chance to follow it."

"Actually, they go on after the next routine," DeMarcus said, his voice calm with a side of *in your face*.

"You sure?" Red-Haired Barbie jumped in. "Kinda hard to dance when you don't have your music."

"The judges already have it," I said. "We gave it to that girl when we registered."

"Oh yeah, we know," Black-Haired Barbie said. "That phone she had looked a lot like mine. So I told her someone must've stolen it. Thanks for turning it in for me."

"What?" Kassie snapped. "That wasn't your phone!"

"Oops. My bad," Black-Haired Barbie said, shrugging. She gave Sarah one last glare of pure evil and walked off with her red-haired twin. I looked at my crew. Doomed. With a capital *D*. No music meant no routine.

"That was a sucky move, Sarah. Even for you," De-Marcus said.

"I had nothing to do with that, I swear," she said, getting a loud *Shhh!* from the backstage volunteer.

"I can spot bad acting from a mile away," Austin said, his eyes narrowed. "She's telling the truth."

"It doesn't matter," Carson said, throwing his arms up and letting them fall. "We can't compete."

"We can just give them my phone," I said. "We'll just use a new song."

Sarah shook her head. "Music can't be turned in after the routines start. It says so in the—wait." She grabbed backstage guy's arm. "They can have someone sing, right?"

"Yeah, but you would've had to notify the judges beforehand," the guy said.

"They don't have time for that! Just give them a mike!"

"Sorry, but—"

"Look!" Sarah snapped into full bossy mode, hip cocked out, arms crossed, one eyebrow up. "My dad's very good friends with the people who run this event and he can make sure you never set foot in the HDC ever again. So go do your job and get them a microphone."

"Um, yes, ma'am," the guy said with a bug-eyed expression smacked onto his face.

Carson nodded. "Not bad."

"Hold on a second. Who's going to sing?" Kassie asked.

Austin threw his hands out in front of him. "Not it."

"You are." Sarah was looking at DeMarcus.

He took a step back. "Wait, no. I can't."

"Yes! This is perfect!" I put my hands on his shoulders as Kassie scribbled *083* on the back of her program. "At the theater. You were awesome."

"But—but that was just for fun. I can't go out and do that onstage."

"Yes, you can. Remember what you told me? Find out who you are and go for it. Maybe this is your chance to do that. Maybe this is your chance to get unstuck."

I could feel him shaking under my hands. He looked at each of us and then took a deep breath. "Okay. I'll do it."

We let out a collective sigh of relief.

"He sings, too?" Carson said to me, fanning his shirt. "This is so unfair."

"So what am I singing?" DeMarcus asked as Sarah pinned the number on his shirt.

"I think I know the perfect song," I said.

DeMarcus smiled, seeming to know exactly what I was thinking. " 'We Will Rock You.' Nice."

"Okay, Freekz. Looks like we're improvising this one," Kassie said, clapping her hands together.

Carson straightened his arms over his head and popped out a perfect spin. "We were born to freestyle."

"*Ninja*-freestyle," I added.

"All we need is a story to tell," Kassie said.

Austin pushed his glasses up his nose. "Step back, ladies and gentlemen. Let the director work his magic."

29

▲▲▲▲▲▲▲▲▲

I was going deaf.

The muffled roar of blood pumping through my head was drowning out everything.

I just hoped DeMarcus's mic would be able to break through it. The lights overhead softened, spreading a thin shadow behind Kassie. She glanced over her shoulder at me and Carson.

A nod.

FUMP! The sound crashed through the speakers as DeMarcus turned the microphone on. He breathed into the mike and paused. Other than a quiet cough from someone in the crowd, it was dead silent. But not for long.

DeMarcus pulled his knee up and brought it back down to start the beat.

Stomp, stomp, CLAP!
Stomp, stomp, CLAP!

It didn't take long for some of the crowd to join in.

For the first part of the song, we just stood there, and every stomp, every clap, became the fuel for our routine. The tension was so thick I could have danced on it. And then just when the audience was about to fall off the edges of their seats, DeMarcus lifted the mike and sang, sending out a shockwave of awesome through the auditorium.

Kassie moved first. She stepped forward and banged out a triple layout. She landed in a front split, right on a big downbeat. Carson was next. He jumped, pulling off a flawless double spin. As soon as he landed, he flew sideways into a cartwheel that ended with him facing Kassie with his arms outstretched, fingers wiggling in full creepy mode.

Time to unleash the Kung Fu Kid.

I let my shoulders fall. My head opened up as every inch of my body soaked in the vocal perfection that poured out of DeMarcus's mouth.

Deep breath.

I felt the music.

I became the music.

The lid snapped shut.

And I was off.

My legs were carrying me toward Kassie at breakneck speed. I jumped over her, clearing her head by a good thirty feet. Or at least that's what it felt like. When I hit the ground, she popped right up and I fell to one knee. Carson jumped toward me. *Punch punch!* I matched every beat with a karate move that would've torn the heads off any villain that got in my way. We were human dance styles, fighting for the dancer in the middle.

I spun on my knees to the right, glancing at Kassie as I did. She whipped her arms through the air, turning, leaping—never the same move twice. Her face was agony, desperation. She sold her part like a pro. I sprang to my feet. Carson's leg stuck out behind him. He brought it down and we exchanged a pair of jabs and kicks.

It was perfect. His pointed-toed, straight-legged, long-necked moves against my lightning-fast flurry of less-than-perfect technique.

He pushed me across the stage. What good's a hero story if the hero doesn't get his butt kicked somewhere? I rolled to the side, crouched. I buried my head in my hands. Hurt. Broken.

Kassie reached out for me. Carson grabbed her arm, pulling her back. She stood in the middle of the stage, busting out a mind-blowing series of breakdance moves while Carson danced around her. His face was angry. Evil. Amazing. If the crowd wasn't loving this, then they were a bunch of robots.

The stage shook with the stomps and claps pouring

from the crowd. It was epic, cramming power into every second of our routine. I imagined it charging my nearly destroyed body as I slowly rose to my feet. A dance phoenix back from the ashes.

I broke into my best hip-hop slide, popping and locking across the stage. Carson spotted me and leaped over, ready to finish the battle.

We tore each other apart. It was a dance to the death. He swirled his arms and legs, looking like a blond-haired ribbon. And I was the ninja sword that'd cut him into shreds. Every spin, every jump, every move I made was pumped full of my favorite martial arts goodness. We fought forever, it seemed, and even almost actually hit each other a couple of times. But in the end, he was defeated. He jumped back, dropping to the floor to dance out his last move—a death scene that would've made any Hollywood actor jealous.

I'd won. The Kung Fu Kid was victorious.

I looked up at Kassie. Our eyes met. Don't ask me how, because I wouldn't be able to tell you, but we spoke. Without saying a word, we spoke to each other. She said, *This is it*, and I replied, *Bring it on*.

I turned, the superhero returning to his lair. Every nerve in my body was on full alert. Like I could feel her running toward me. She came closer. And when it was time, she didn't signal me. No yelling—I just knew.

I spun around. She was airborne. Time hit a wall that

slowed it down like it was backflipping through maple syrup. There wasn't a single detail of Kassie I didn't see.

Her eyes with the white speckles of the spotlight reflecting in them.

Her hair flying out behind her, trying to catch up.

Her arms outstretched toward me.

DeMarcus had to still be singing. But I didn't hear anything. No song. No crowd. Just the pounding of my heart. I wondered if Kassie heard it, too.

Then the slow-motion effect sped back up and reality came crashing back into full speed. I wasn't ready for it, because when Kassie slammed against my chest, my entire body rocked backward. I flung my arms around her as she wrapped both legs around my waist. My shoes barked out a loud screech. I tried to keep my balance. I spun, hoping that would keep me from falling.

Our faces were so close. They'd never been that close. Ever. I'd hugged Kassie a million times, but this was more than just a hug. She was holding me. Before I knew what I was doing, my lips puckered. I couldn't stop them. It was like they'd torn themselves away from my brain. They were going in for a kiss and there was nothing I could do.

The smile on Kassie's face faded. Her eyes bulged. I tried to reel my mouth back into non-fish-lips mode, but they were on a mission. A mission I didn't even send them on. I was about to force an *I'm sorry!* out through them, but before I could, Kassie leaned forward.

Right into my kiss!

Her eyes closed just as mine popped open even wider.

Our lips touched. And on purpose. For a second all I could think was how there was no "How to Kiss a Girl" section of my dance tutorials. But in an instant that was gone. My brain exploded, fireworks shooting out of my ears and white doves flying out of the top of my head.

My elbow clipped the edge of the side curtain. I stepped back. Right onto my shoelace. There were stumbles. Lots of them. But only one fall. It only took one to completely ruin the Kiss. It only took one fall to totally destroy the lift that was going to win us that competition.

I never hit the ground, though. I should have. My first thought was that I was falling off the actual stage, but I wasn't. Kassie had her feet shoved into the floor with her hands clamped around my wrists.

She caught me.

The crowd roared out a mixture of applause and cheers. But Kassie wasn't smiling. Her face was stuck in panic mode. Carson ran over to us and a few seconds later DeMarcus was there, too. We scrambled offstage to meet Austin, laughing and all talking at once. Except for Kassie. Surely our moment hadn't been that bad. I'd never win a trophy in a kissing contest, but I'd do better than coming in dead last.

"That was insane!" Carson yelled. "For a second I

thought you two kissed! Oh my gosh, that would've been incredible. Can you image if you'd kissed her?"

Kassie and I glanced at each other. They'd missed it. Probably because I was in the middle of falling to my death at the time. Kassie rubbed the back of her neck, looking nervous. "Um, so the song—it sounded amazing, DeMarcus."

"Dude, that was better than awesome! That was beast!" Austin added.

"Thanks, guys. Sorry I paused at the end. I thought you fell."

"We did," I said, laughing. But it was forced. My mind was somewhere else. Somewhere stuck between a pair of lips.

The next group trotted out onstage in perfect unison and we scooted farther back into the shadows of the backstage area. As everyone walked away, I pulled Kassie to the side.

"Hey, is everything okay?"

She pulled her arms up against her, crossing them tight against her stomach. "Yeah, um, I'm fine."

Her eyes were everywhere except on mine. Something was wrong. It didn't take a genius to put the pieces together, either.

"Look . . ." I took a deep breath. "Back there, during the lift. I didn't mean to—"

"I know," she interrupted. "I know you didn't. I'm sorry. I really am."

Her eyes dropped. My mind raced, wondering what she was sorry for. I was the one who'd messed up.

"It just sorta . . . happened."

Kassie nodded. "We were just caught up in the story, I guess."

"Guys, let's go!" Carson said, running up to us. "The announcer said awards are next!" He grabbed Kassie's wrist and they jogged off toward the wings, where the other dancers were gathering.

It took a second for my feet to get moving. I wanted to be back on that stage. With Kassie's arms around me. With her lips touching mine.

Kassie was wrong. It wasn't just part of the act. It wasn't just part of the story.

It was real.

30

▲▲▲▲▲▲▲▲▲

The stage creaked under our weight.

Nearly every dancer was crammed behind the announcer. We were stuck standing in the corner. Every time my shoulder touched Kassie's, it made me jump. I forced my eyes straight ahead, out to the audience. I tried to find Austin or DeMarcus, but it was impossible. There were a million spotlights pointed at us and all I could see in front of me was the outline of the guy with the mike. I looked across the stage, where the other older groups were. A flash of a red ponytail caught my eye. The Barbies. Sarah was standing right beside them, her head up a little higher than usual.

But she wasn't wearing the better-than-everyone look she usually had on.

No, right then she just looked proud of herself.

And after the way she had danced, she totally should've been.

"Ladies and gentlemen," the announcer said. "We're going to open our ceremony tonight with the showcase awards." The crowd went crazy.

When it got quiet, he started reading the winners from categories like Best Costume (080—the cowboy routine), Best Use of Props (031—one of those exercise balls painted up to look like a giant ball of yarn), and the one I thought should've gone to us, Best Music (053—a techno version of "Rocky Top").

Next were the scholarships. Heartland awarded some of their own to soloists in the different age divisions, and four studios had their own to hand out. Dance-Splosion was last. The announcer looked down at his paper. "And finally, the winner of Dance-Splosion's three-week scholarship is . . . Avery Yates!"

The audience applauded as Avery walked out to stand beside him. Carson put a hand on my shoulder and gave it a squeeze. I saw Sarah clapping, getting even more dirty looks from her Barbies. She glanced across the stage at me and we shared a quick smile. Part of me wondered if my name had ever been on that certificate. The same part of me was worrying about it less and less. My mom and dad would have a million questions about the scholarship. But I also knew I finally had all the answers to them.

The lobby door opened and I caught Kenton walking

out. I imagined him pitching a fit outside. Maybe he'd even do one of those clear-the-entire-table-with-one-swipe-of-the-hands routines. Then maybe he'd get arrested and thrown in jail for being a jerk.

The announcer finally moved on to the dance awards. He began with the winners in the Mini Division. The crowd cheered like crazy for every winner. Ours would be the last one, which meant there was more time for the stomach-tied-in-a-knot nervousness to grow.

About the award.

About whether or not Mom and Dad had noticed I hadn't worn my tights.

Most of all, though, about the Kiss.

I tried to pull my thoughts away, but I couldn't. Every time I'd glance over at Kassie, she'd look away.

The announcer called off the awards in the Junior Division.

"Guys," Carson whispered, "I think we actually have a shot at this!"

"Like winning? You mean a trophy?" I asked.

"Why not? We were top-five material at least."

Kassie and I glanced at each other, the awkward tension frozen between us.

"Ladies and gentlemen, now for our last round of awards," the announcer said. "The Teen Division."

A rumble of polite claps from the audience. Solo and duet winners were announced first, fifth place and working backward up to first. Trios and small-group awards were next.

"Remember, guys," Carson said, eyes closed. "This is our first big competition. Fifth place is like first for us."

The announcer raised the mike. "Our fifth-place winner is . . . number 68, *Winter's Playground!*"

Carson squeezed my hand harder.

"Our fourth-place winner is . . . number 49, *The Moment It All Began!*"

My breathing sped up. We'd blown some minds with our routine, but could we have actually placed in the top three?

"Our third-place winner is . . . number 55, *Running Forever!*"

Sweat beaded up on my forehead.

"Our second-place winner is . . . number 81, *Because of You!*"

Sarah's group. I couldn't believe it didn't win. We clapped—Carson louder than all of us. The Barbies strutted upstage in front of Sarah.

"And, ladies and gentlemen, now for our last award of the evening."

My stomach tightened. I looked at my crew. I could tell they were thinking the same thing I was. That this could be it. That we could be the next ones called up. That we might've beaten every odd, dancing a totally improvised routine with no costumes and a middle school quarterback singing our song for us. I played the movie version of the moment in my head, hearing the judge call our number, seeing Kassie hold the gigantic golden trophy over her head, feeling her lips touch mine one more time.

I took a deep breath and trained my eyes back on the announcer.

"Our overall high-scoring routine in the group and line production category is . . ."

The beat of silence that came next lasted forever. The entire stage was frozen still like everyone was holding their breath. We all waited. That agonizing moment where the announcer teased our patience, dangling the name of the winner in front of us just out of reach.

And then he raised the mike and spoke. "Number 84—"

My heart stopped. My mind screamed, *That's us! That's our number!*

"*Out of This World!*" the announcer shouted.

But that wasn't our routine. What was going on? I glanced down at the sticker on my shirt and I was judo-chopped back to reality. We were 83.

We'd lost.

31

▲▲▲▲▲▲▲▲▲

The stage rumbled under the stampede of dancers.

Loud music blared over the speakers as everyone made their way back into the audience. The edge of a trophy caught the spotlight and reflected it right into my eye, like a slap across the face to say, *Neener, neener, you can't win me.*

Austin threw a pudgy leg over the edge of the stage and climbed up. "Hey, guys," he said, out of breath. "You were totally robbed."

I let out a long breath. "If—"

"Nope," Kassie said. "Not gonna hear it."

My eyebrows tensed up. "What?"

"I know what you're going to say, Dillon. *If I were a better dancer, we would've won.*"

"Who cares if we lost?" Carson said. "We got out there and rocked their little worlds with our routine."

I lifted my hand, ready to speak, but Austin jumped in. "Plus that trophy looked pretty lame anyway."

"See," Kassie said, grabbing my shoulders. "We don't care. So no more excuses. You're as good a dancer as anyone else in this auditorium." She ended her speech with a quick nod, crossing her arms.

I pushed my hair away from my eyes and hid the smile creeping up my mouth. "Actually, I was gonna say if Carson wants to go ahead and change, I'll take my tights back."

They looked at each other and burst into laughter.

"But thanks anyway. And thanks for letting me back in. And for not hating me for acting so crazy this year," I said. "Thanks for everything, actually. If it wasn't for you all, I probably wouldn't even *be* a dancer."

"Yeah you would," Kassie said. "You were born to dance. And I have to admit, your technique was looking pretty good out there."

My ears got warm all of a sudden. I tried to shove my hands in my pockets, but my football pants didn't have any. So I just stood there, red-faced and goofy, smiling at her.

But the smile jumped off my face when I spotted DeMarcus talking to Sarah at the edge of the stage. He was holding her hands. For a second I thought maybe he was apologizing for something. The way he was shaking his head as he talked told me a different story. They were breaking up. But not your typical angsty-teen-movie breakup. No screaming. No arm flailing. No tears. She just gave him a hug.

When Sarah walked back toward the wing, her dad was standing there, holding her jacket. I don't know how, but I knew she was going to be okay. She'd told her dad exactly what she needed to onstage.

DeMarcus planted a hand on my shoulder. "Hey, guys. First of all"—he held out a finger—"we were totally robbed."

"Exactly!" Austin yelled, tossing his hands in the air.

"I know, right? That part with the jump? Man, that was like—" He put his hands beside his head and mimed his brain exploding.

Carson clapped. "Good. Totally my idea, if you remember."

"Definitely." He held out another finger and turned to Kassie. "Second, do you think I could talk to you? Just for a minute?"

"Sure." She walked off with him. He whispered something in her ear.

My insides turned to ice. What was happening? I was almost totally sure he'd just broken up with Sarah. And now he wanted to talk to Kassie?

I may not have had the movie moment I wanted during

the awards, but I wasn't about to let this one get ruined. "Wait!" I yelled. Kassie and DeMarcus turned around. "I have to talk to Kassie, too. About something. It's important."

"I'll be right back," she said, laughing.

"Yeah, but—I can't— It's important, Kass."

"So is this, Dillon. Give me like one minute, okay?" She turned back around and they continued to talk, too soft to hear. Not that I'd *want* to.

It was over. My stomach knotted up so hard I nearly fell. Carson caught my attention with a little wave. He put his hand to his mouth and pretended to lock the corner.

What? Why was he telling me to shut up? I couldn't. Not now. He rolled his eyes, twisting the imaginary key again. And then opened his mouth. No, he wasn't locking—he was *unlocking.*

Austin shoved his face right next to my ear, whispering, "Dude, just get over there and tell her how you feel."

They were right. I'd done enough waiting. My heart sped up. *Don't just stand there, dummy. Unlock before she's gone forever.*

Before I could figure out how, Austin pushed me forward. My feet planted and a grunt pushed its way out past my lips along with three words.

"I like you!"

Kassie's head shot around DeMarcus. "What?"

I looked back at Carson and Austin. They were standing shoulder to shoulder, nodding like a pair of bobbleheads. Carson had his arm latched onto Austin's.

When I turned back around, DeMarcus was staring at me, too. My fingers wrapped themselves in the end of my shirt. "I'm sorry I'm saying this now, but—no, I'm not sorry, actually."

I took a step forward. Kassie and DeMarcus gave each other a quick look.

"DeMarcus, you're an awesome guy. You helped me out in football and you pretty much saved our crew today, but I can't let you do this. Not yet."

His eyebrows shot up, surprised. Kassie glanced around nervously, her eyes finally stopping on me.

"I should've said this sooner. I know I may have already lost my chance, but I don't care. Maybe I'm too late and you're already DeMarcus's girlfriend now, but that doesn't change anything. I like you, Kass. Like, *really* like you. And I think I have for a long time, too. I just never had the guts to say anything until tonight."

She looked away. Maybe embarrassed. Maybe shocked. I couldn't tell. I took a deep breath, waiting for more words to come together in my head.

"You've always taught me that every time we dance, we're making up some new world we wanna live in and sharing that with everyone. And it's our job to come up with the perfect story."

My arm weighed a ton, but I forced it up, holding my hand out to her.

"I think we'd make a pretty good one."

Behind me, someone let out a breathy *Awww!* And they should've, because that came out a lot smoother than I thought it would. I was feeling pretty good, but it didn't last long. Kassie bit the edge of her lip. She looked at DeMarcus. Not me, but him. I swallowed a gigantic lump in my throat. I understood.

Kassie had made her choice.

DeMarcus beamed a warm smile at me. I hated it. Part of me wanted to reach up and tear it off his face. But I wouldn't. If there was one guy besides me who deserved to be with Kassie, it was him.

"Actually I was talking to her about . . ." He glanced past me. The skin around his cheeks darkened. "Okay, so for a while now I've liked someone, too. And I wasn't sure how to tell them, either. But since I met you guys and saw how you all did your own thing, it sort of gave me, I don't know . . . confidence, I guess."

Seriously? Sunnydale's star quarterback needed some confidence to steal Kassie away from me?

My hand was still stretched out to Kassie. I pulled it back. "Glad we could help, I guess." My feet felt like they were buried in concrete, but I managed to turn. As I did, I forced a smile at Kassie and whispered, "I hope I didn't embarrass you."

I'd only taken one step when DeMarcus breezed by me. Without Kassie in his arms. He walked right up to Carson and said something to him.

My entire body went rigid. The same way it does when I see a stink bug in my house. But this wasn't fear. It was that moment your body tenses up right before the feeling of pure relief kicks in.

Carson's entire face had gone even paler than it usually was. His eyes were bulging and his jaw was hanging open. Then a smile formed on his mouth and he nodded.

DeMarcus wasn't lying about having a secret crush on someone.

And it was Carson all along.

Suddenly a lot of things made sense. Why DeMarcus never seemed all swoony over Sarah. Why Sarah kept mentioning things like his reputation. Even why she got all weird over Carson taking his picture. Everyone sort of expects a dancer could be gay. The quarterback with the cannon? Yeah, not so much.

I guessed she was just trying to get him to play by the rules, too.

But maybe some things weren't supposed to have rules. And if there were, maybe some rules were supposed to be broken.

Someone grabbed my wrist. I looked down at Kassie's fingers locking over mine. Every cell in my hand exploded in a firework of happiness. The surge of electricity rushed up my arm into my chest, making the already-manic butterflies in my stomach go nuts.

Kassie smiled. "I'm *really* glad we added in that lift."

We both laughed. That single stray curl hung down over one of her eyes. I reached up and tucked it behind her ear.

"Yeah. Me too."

Austin was beside my parents, recording the whole thing with his phone. "This is totally going in the music video!"

I looked back at Kassie and we laughed. *Go ahead and post it,* I thought. *No masks. This is one I don't care if the world sees.*

32

▲▲▲▲▲▲▲▲▲

On Monday, I walked into the school, ready to get the first half of my seventh-grade year over with.

I hadn't even gotten halfway to my locker before *Tighty Whitey* started rolling off people's lips. I wasn't surprised. When you flash the entire digital world, it has a tendency to be something people don't forget.

But that was okay. There was a pretty good chance I'd be retiring my blue shirt for an actual jersey. And maybe a pair of unstained football pants.

I walked down that hallway, hearing my nickname bounce around from one person to the next. There was still part of me that wondered what people would be saying if I'd won all those free lessons at Dance-Splosion. But that thought was slowly dying away. I actually didn't mind being known as someone who danced his jeans off.

On my way to lunch, I spotted Sarah with her Barbies. She had her nose in the air like she ruled the place. I wondered if we'd ever talk again. I didn't think we would. Eighth-grade club presidents didn't associate with moppy-haired seventh graders with pimples on their chin after all.

But as I passed her by, I caught her eyes. She smiled. Not a *Hey, buddy, come over here and hang out with me and my lipstick legion!* No, it was just a quick grin. A little moment we shared like we were keeping our own secret from the whole world.

And in a way, we were, I guess.

The best part of the day was actually getting to eat lunch with my friends. Without Patrick and his hipster crew. We even saved a seat for DeMarcus. But he didn't sit down.

"Thanks, guys." He glanced over his shoulder at the football table. Sarah was there. "But maybe I should—"

He was interrupted by a pair of low, gravelly giggles.

"Hey, is this the official gay table now?" Bobby said, stopping right behind DeMarcus.

Before DeMarcus could say anything, Troy stepped forward. "Kaylee showed us your little video. You and your boyfriend holding hands."

Austin let out a groan. It must've been the one he posted. DeMarcus opened his mouth like he was going to say something, but then shut it.

"That why you decided to play football in the first place?" Troy asked. "To watch us in the locker room?"

DeMarcus and Troy both lowered their trays, and for a second I was sure they were going to throw them down and start pounding on each other. Bobby slithered up beside them, smiling like the idea of a fight was the most exciting thing ever.

But then DeMarcus shook his head. "Whatever, man." He sat down, his eyes never leaving the table in front of him.

Troy finally took a step back. "Better be glad football season's over. I never would've blocked all them guys from running over you if I'd known."

Bobby grunted out a laugh and walked off behind Troy.

For a while we just sat there. Quiet.

Then DeMarcus peeled open his milk. "Not like he did an awesome job of blocking before now anyway."

I laughed with everyone else, but it felt awkward and forced. Austin buried his head in his hands. "Dude, I'm so sorry. I should've asked before I posted it. I didn't even think. Please don't hate me."

"I don't. Really."

"Those guys are idiots," Kassie said.

Carson nodded. "I can think of a few stronger words. What they said was horrible."

I looked past DeMarcus at the football table. Troy and

Bobby were still laughing. Some of the other football players had joined in, but a few were picking up their trays and moving to another table. Led by Sarah.

"Carson's right," I said. "Those two don't know what they're talking about."

"I know. It's kinda weird, though. People have been looking at me and whispering. I know they know, but—" DeMarcus sighed. "I feel okay. Scared, yeah. But better than I've felt in a while, actually."

Carson smiled. "You know we'll always have your back."

"Hey, you think we have room for an honorary member?" I asked Kassie. "I think he's earned it, don't you?"

Her eyes lit up. "Totally." She took off her Dizzee Freekz pin and handed it to DeMarcus. "I know it doesn't make up for what those two said, but Dillon's right. You earned it. You found the moves that fit you. Welcome to the crew."

He stared at the pin, grinning. "Thank you." He stuck it on his shirt and sat up a little straighter. "All of you."

We spent the rest of lunch checking out our music video. Austin cringed a little at the part he'd added in with DeMarcus and Carson, but DeMarcus just laughed and asked him why he didn't get more screen time.

The video already had four comments. And the first one? Avery. It was practically a novel. I got some weird looks from everyone when she mentioned how thankful she was for my string. But when we got to the part about how she thought we were robbed (getting another "Exactly!" from Austin) and how DeMarcus did such an awesome job, Kassie came up with the idea for him to sing with our crew from then on.

He said yes.

We'd be the first middle school dance crew with a singing quarterback.

When everyone was at my house for practice that Saturday, Dad brought a letter downstairs. It was from a place I'd never heard of: the Knoxville Dance Academy. Even though it was addressed to me, the top of the letter had all of our names on it.

"Dude, maybe it's another competition!" Austin said, snatching the envelope out of my hands. I stood beside him as he ripped it open. A familiar fluttery tickle of excitement hatched in my gut.

"Cool! I'd be up for that," DeMarcus said.

"No way," Austin said as I scanned the first few lines. "This is totally better! It's—"

"Nothing. Not a competition." I took the letter and stuffed it back in the envelope, the tingling sensation in my stomach fizzling out.

"Well, what is it, then?" Carson grabbed for it.

"It's nothing," I said, pulling it out of his reach. "Trust me."

He grabbed for it again. "I saw my name at the top,

too. Now hand it over before I go all spider monkey on you."

Kassie laughed and yanked the envelope away from me.

"Kass, don't—" It was too late. She already had it out, reading it. Her smile faded.

"Oh my gosh, are you all trying to torture me?" Carson asked. "What does it say?"

Kassie let her hands fall against her legs. "It's an invitation. For some free classes at a new studio."

Carson's hands shot to his mouth like he'd just won best performance at the Tony Awards.

I looked at the letter in Kassie's hands. I could just make out the studio director's picture—Mrs. Smiley. "Like I said, it's nothing." I reached out to take it back.

Kassie pulled it up in front of her. "They're asking us to go to this place for an entire week. Apparently it's some new sister studio of Dance-Splosion's."

The mood in the room went south. And fast. Even DeMarcus lowered his eyes like he was having a moment of silence for the opportunity.

"You all know my rule. My *only* rule. Right?"

We nodded. I felt like a boot camp soldier about to be chewed out by a drill sergeant.

"Good," she said, walking over to me. It took every bit of energy I had just to look her in the eyes. And when I did, I saw something hiding in there. A smile. She took my hand, putting the letter back in it. "Then maybe we can all agree how stupid it is."

My eyes popped open. Austin blurted out exactly what I was thinking. "Is dating Dill, like, messing with your brain or something?"

"Shush, Austin. And no, it's not." She shrugged, her eyes falling to the letter. "I just—maybe I wasn't being fair with that rule. I had a bad experience at a studio, sure. And I'm beginning to think it wasn't totally their fault. I might've been a little stubborn back then."

"Back then?" Carson said.

Kassie stuck her tongue out at him. "What I'm saying is, my whole deal was how I thought Dance-Splosion was forcing me to learn new moves. I guess, in a way, I was doing the same thing by keeping Dillon from learning what he wanted to learn."

At that exact second, my heart nearly exploded, because that's when every *I like you, Kassie* feeling I had turned into something even bigger.

"Dillon totally gave up a shot at doing something he wanted because of that rule. I'm not going to let that happen again."

She gave me a quick kiss on my cheek and my entire face died and went to heaven.

"If this is a trick or something, I'll cry," Carson said. "And it'll be ugly, too, I swear."

Kassie shook her head. "It's not a trick."

"You mean we're going for it?" Austin asked.

"It's not my decision. Not this time." Kassie looked at me like she was waiting for me to answer. So was everyone else.

That's when it happened. A tingle worked its way up my legs and crawled over my body like a warm blanket.

My liftoff out of the wannabe-dancer universe.

And not because we had a week of studio classes in our sights. It was because right then—with all of my friends looking at me—I didn't care if we danced in that studio or stuck to making up our own routines in a smelly basement. All I wanted to do was dance.

I took a deep breath. "As long as we get to dance together, I'm happy."

The basement ceiling nearly caved in from our cheers.

We got into our positions and I felt better than I'd ever felt in my life. The music started and my head-lid opened up, ready to soak up the fuel my body needed. And as soon as I rocked out my first flurry of punches and kicks with the straightest lines I'd ever had . . .

I finally understood it all.

Studios aren't the enemy. But they're not the only answer, either. Sure, the technique is important. So are the rules. They're not there to hold you back. They're there to help you do the *really* important stuff:

To tell the story you want to tell with your dance.

My dad had told me that every team needs its support

players. And for the longest time, I sort of assumed that the support players were the ones who weren't really needed. They were the "just in case" people.

But they're more than that. They're the "just as important as" people.

They might not be the same, but they're still needed. Like the people in the Army Reserves. Like the blue shirts. Like me.

It took me almost half a school year and three pairs of tights to finally understand. But I got there. And I wasn't about to go back. Maybe I'd never get rid of Tighty Whitey. But that was okay. I was more than just that.

I was a member of the Dizzee Freekz.

I was the Kung Fu Kid.

I was Dillon Parker, the dancer.

A *real* dancer.

ACKNOWLEDGMENTS

I've had so many amazing partners throughout this process. I've been learning a whole new routine during this journey and you've all made sure I haven't had to learn it alone. So to every person I've shared the literary floor with in one way or another, I can't thank you enough.

But that won't stop me from trying.

To Jackie—my best friend and wife: thank you for never giving up on me while I stumbled my way through my first draft. And the second. And third. Our "writing walks" were always amazing, and your suggestions were never taken lightly. There's as much of you in this book as there is of me.

To my amazing supporters, critique partners, beta readers, and anyone who helped me better a word, sentence, or character—Jason Benjamin, Sasha Benjamin, Cristina Moreno, Dr. Wooten, Amber Mauldin, Jayme Woods, Jenna Lehne, Jessie Devine, Sean McConnell, Dayla F. M., Brenda Drake, Dannie Morin, Heidi

Schulz, Melanie Conklin, Ronni Arno Blaisdell, Jean Giardina, Karen Lee Hallam, Jeff Chen, Gail Nall, Jen Malone, Marieke Nijkamp, Joy McCullough-Carranza, Brent Taylor, Patrice Caldwell, Genetta Adair, Taryn Albright, Juliana Brandt, Lauren Spieller, Brianna Shrum, Dave Connis, the Sweet Sixteens debut author group, the MG Beta Readers team, and the Middle Grade Minded team: thank you for cheering me on, letting me try out new steps with my stories, and never hesitating to tell me when they weren't working.

To the Midsouth SCBWI—the folks who organize the events, the speakers who have given their time to it, and Gail for introducing me to literally every single person during my first conference: thank you for motivating me to stop standing in the wings and to take my manuscript out on the floor.

To Mom and Dad: thank you for always letting me be goofy and creative. I think you would've loved this story.

To LeeLoo: thank you for keeping the barking to a minimum during the edits.

To my fellow New Kidz: thank you for always showing up after school to practice. Even though we all chickened out and canceled our end-of-the-year show for the school, we still had fun trying to figure out how to spin on our heads.

To Kate Gartner and The Little Friends of Printmaking, JW and Melissa Buchanan: thank you for your incredible eye for artistic detail. I couldn't have asked for a more perfect cover!

To Jen at *Pop! Goes the Reader:* thank you for giving my cover reveal a place to call home.

To Uwe Stender and the TriadaUS team: thank you for your undying enthusiasm and love for these characters. I never doubted that the Dizzee Freekz were safe in your hands.

To Wendy Loggia and the Delacorte Press team: thank you for your remarkable insight and guidance. You championed this story and helped me transform it into something better than I ever thought it could be.

And finally, to my readers: I hope you found a little of yourself in this book, too. Thank you for taking a chance on the Dizzee Freekz. You're all honorary members for life.

ABOUT THE AUTHOR

In sixth grade, Brooks Benjamin formed a New Kids on the Block tribute dance crew called the New Kidz. He wasn't that good at dancing back then. But now he's got a new crew—his wife and their dog. They live in Tennessee, where he teaches reading and writing and occasionally busts out a few dance moves. He's still not very good at it.

Visit Brooks Benjamin online at
brooksbenjamin.com

Follow Brooks Benjamin on